THE

QUARTERLY

EDITED BY

GORDON LISH

Dear "Editor";
  Thank You for the nice ink
pens you sent me so my letters
will look better in your magazine,
I'm so happy, I am "famous".
            Your friend,
            Enid J. Crackel (Mrs.)

According to Diane DeSanders, "Maybe She Sings" made the rounds. According to Ms. DeSanders, "Maybe She Sings" could find no taker anywhere—until *The Quarterly* took. One wonders what might be made of this. Can one say that literary standards elsewhere are more exacting than they are at *The Quarterly*? Or are standards just alibis for desire? We desired "Maybe She Sings," and took it, but our doing so did nothing to take the edge off our desire. On the contrary, the success we have been enjoying in gaining what we desire has made us even more wildly the creature of our appetite. *The Quarterly* wants. *The Quarterly* wants what it never has had. What *The Quarterly* wants is very likely an object not wanted anywhere else. Good. Such a state of affairs is exactly what *The Quarterly* requires. Our desire is colossal—and would go hopelessly unanswered if other magazines were given to desiring what we desire. Swell—it looks as if they are not. As for standards, we will be happy to hit ours with a hammer if they appear to be trying to get in the way of our making room for what we know we need. Enter "Maybe She Sings"—right where our readers cannot miss it, right where it roundly is.

THE QUARTERLY

15 / FALL 1990

VINTAGE BOOKS

A DIVISION OF RANDOM HOUSE, INC.

NEW YORK

COPYRIGHT © 1990 BY THE QUARTERLY
ALL RIGHTS RESERVED UNDER INTERNATIONAL AND PAN-AMERICAN
COPYRIGHT CONVENTIONS. PUBLISHED IN THE UNITED STATES BY VINTAGE BOOKS,
A DIVISION OF RANDOM HOUSE, INC., NEW YORK, AND SIMULTANEOUSLY IN
CANADA BY RANDOM HOUSE OF CANADA LIMITED, TORONTO.

THE QUARTERLY (ISSN: 0893-3103) IS EDITED BY GORDON LISH
AND IS PUBLISHED MARCH, JUNE, SEPTEMBER, AND DECEMBER BY
VINTAGE BOOKS, A DIVISION OF RANDOM HOUSE, INC.,
201 EAST 50TH STREET, NEW YORK, NY 10022. SUBSCRIPTIONS—
FOUR ISSUES AT $40 US, $54 CANADIAN, $46 US OVERSEAS—AND ADDRESS
CHANGES SHOULD BE SENT TO THE ATTENTION OF SUBSCRIPTION OFFICE,
28TH FLOOR. ORDERS RECEIVED BY JANUARY 31 START WITH MARCH NUMBER;
BY APRIL 30, JUNE NUMBER; BY JULY 31, SEPTEMBER NUMBER; BY OCTOBER 31,
DECEMBER NUMBER. SEE LAST PAGE FOR PURCHASE OF BACK NUMBERS.

MANAGEMENT BY ELLEN F. TORRON
EDITORIAL ASSISTANCE BY RICK WHITAKER

THE QUARTERLY WELCOMES THE OPPORTUNITY TO READ WORK OF EVERY
CHARACTER, AND IS ESPECIALLY CONCERNED TO KEEP ITSELF AN OPEN FORUM.
MANUSCRIPTS MUST BE ACCOMPANIED BY THE CUSTOMARY RETURN MATERIALS, AND
SHOULD BE ADDRESSED TO THE EDITOR, THE QUARTERLY, 201 EAST 50TH STREET,
NEW YORK, NY 10022. THE QUARTERLY MAKES THE UTMOST EFFORT TO OFFER ITS
RESPONSE TO MANUSCRIPTS NO LATER THAN ONE WEEK SUBSEQUENT TO RECEIPT.
OPINIONS EXPRESSED HEREIN ARE NOT NECESSARILY THOSE OF THE EDITOR OR OF
THE PUBLISHER.

ISBN: 0-679-73231-4

DESIGN BY ANDREW ROBERTS
INSTALLATION BY DENISE STEWART

O ART DIRECTOR, ART DIRECTOR! FOR THE EDITOR REMEMBERS ALL TOO TELLINGLY
THE YEARS WHEN HE LOITERED IN THE CORRIDORS OF ESQUIRE MAGAZINE AND HAD,
FOR HIS WATCHFUL LABORS, NO LITTLE INSTRUCTION IN THE SORROWS
SUBSUMED UNDER THE TITLE ART DIRECTOR. MORE TELLINGLY STILL,
THE EDITOR IS ABLE TO MAKE THE BOAST OF HIS HAVING, FOR HIS SINS,
A SPOUSE WHO WAS AN ART DIRECTOR. BUT NOWHERE IN THE KEN OF THE EDITOR
IS THERE AN ART DIRECTOR MORE VEXED THAN THIS ART DIRECTOR, THAN
THE EDITOR'S ART DIRECTOR, THAN THE QUARTERLY'S ART DIRECTOR!—
THE FORBEARING, FORGIVING CATHRYN S. AISON, LONG MAY SHE ARTFULLY (EVEN,
IF SHE MUST, DIRECTORALLY) WAVE!

MANUFACTURED IN THE UNITED STATES OF AMERICA

THE QUARTERLY

15 / FALL 1990

A NACE PAGE   2

DIANE DESANDERS / *Maybe She Sings*   3

DON DELILLO / *The Rapture of the Athlete Assumed into Heaven*   6

PATRICIA LEAR / *Hot*   8

SAM MICHEL / *The Beast, Watered*   13

WALTER KIRN / *The Orphan*   17

NOY HOLLAND / *He Has Been to Macy's*   27

J. R. RODRIGUEZ / *Soil*   34

DENNIS VANNATTA / *Mothers*   38

DEREK GULLINO / *Three Fictions*   48

GARY AMDAHL / *The Bouncers*   59

KATHERINE ARNOLDI / *Crosscut Saw*   72

DIANE WILLIAMS / *Three Fictions*   75

RAY HALLIDAY / *Right Out of a Machine*   78

HUGH KELLEHER / *A History of My Life*   81

GREG MULCAHY / *Fishing Trips*   83

MARTIN SHERMAN / *The Story*   89

EVELYN KONRAD / *The Son*   94

RICHARD BLANCHARD / *Travelers*   96

MACDONALD HARRIS / *Old L.A.*   98

THE QUARTERLY

RICK WHITAKER / *Drives* *101*

PHILIP GOUREVITCH / *War Story* *102*

JACQUELYN REINGOLD / *The Men Who Wanted
to Be President* *104*

AMY GODINE / *Mercy* *107*

DAWN RAFFEL / *Delivery* *165*

BARBARA BLEWER / *Run in Place* *166*

MICHAEL HICKINS / *Affair* *171*

ANOTHER NACE PAGE *178*

BRUCE BOND *179*

STEPHEN HICKOFF *189*

EMMA DONOGHUE *190*

MICHAEL HEFFERNAN *192*

COOPER ESTEBAN *194*

JONAH WINTER *204*

JOE AHEARN *206*

ELLIOT RICHMAN *207*

MICHELLE RHEA *210*

TIMOTHY LIU *212*

ANSIE BAIRD *214*

EDMUND CONTI *216*

JOHN RYBICKI   217

RACHEL LODEN   219

ONE MORE NACE PAGE   220

PAULETTE JILES *to* Q   221

ENID CRACKEL *to* Q   225

RUSSELL SHORTO *to* Q   226

ENID CRACKEL *to* Q   229

SHARON KORSHAK *to* Q   230

TOM AHERN *to* Q   232

PATRICIA MARX *to* Q   233

YUNG LUNG *to* Q   236

ENID CRACKEL *to* Q   239

TOM AHERN *to* Q   240

PAULETTE JILES *to* Q   241

FRANCIS LEVY *to* Q   244

THE LAST NACE PAGE   246

THE
QUARTERLY

I would go to New York

Maybe She Sings

My daughter plays Superman. She gets out there in that apartment-complex back yard with the trash cans and the clotheslines and the conditional grass crisscrossed by a dozen narrow sidewalks, and my daughter runs around with a dish towel pinned to her last-summer's-bathing-suit straps, the bathing suit pulled on over cotton tights and a T-shirt and emblazoned with a paper-cutout yellow-and-red-Crayola'd **S** pinned on the chest.

S for Superman.

Actually, running around is not what my daughter does out there. I keep an eye on her from the kitchen window of our downstairs apartment when I get home from school and work and pay the babysitter—and I'm thinking of something cheap for dinner, like hot dogs or Campbell's soup or scrambled eggs for the two of us so I can get us fed and ready for bed early so I can study at night.

I never see my daughter running out there with her arms out, or jumping off the steps to pretend flying, the way it seems to me I would do if I were a little kid almost four years old playing Superman. I mean, my daughter seems to me to be so serious about it.

Maybe my daughter runs and jumps when I'm not looking, when no one's around. Maybe my daughter runs and jumps and skips and dances all around the yard when there is no one there to see her. Maybe my daughter sings. But all I know is that there she is, walking around the yard talking to herself. Well, talking to someone I bet she's imagining as part of whatever story she is telling herself out there. She stands next to a large bush and talks into it. She talks to a dog that seems to me to be just passing through. She goes up on the cement back steps of the apartment directly opposite ours—across the yard.

I see my daughter stand up there on the steps with her baby-fat hands on her almost-four-year-old hips. She looks out at the yard. I see the paper **S** flutter a bit on her chest. My daughter stands up there for a time on the steps in what I suppose to be her best Superman fashion, as if to say, "This is the yard and I am its ruler." Then I see her stepping down the steps.

There are five of them.

She still takes them one at a time.

I open a can of Vienna sausages to throw in with the scrambled eggs. I get out some bread to make cinnamon toast for dessert. We'll have to live on what's already in the kitchen for the rest of the month again.

I hear a cry, look out, see my daughter fallen down out there on the sidewalk. (Could she have been running?) She's crying and looking back this way. The yellow-and-red-paper **S** has torn off, and she's holding it out to me, reaching her arm outstretched to its almost-four-year-old reach, her head to one side.

I call out to her. "Come on in now!" I say. "You're fine!" I say. "Come on in and I'll fix it for you!"

She watches *Outer Limits,* with her cinnamon toast, the Superman **S** pinned onto her pajamas, while I sit in the bathtub in the next room with the door ajar so I can hear whatever's going on. I don't know. Maybe I shouldn't let her watch a show that scares her so much. But she gets so upset about wanting to see it—as if it really means something to her to be able to sit through that show. And so I let her watch. "Jack and the Beanstalk" scares her just as much.

Sometimes I sit in the bathtub for a long time. Sometimes I spend an entire evening in the bathtub, just sitting or lying and staring into space. A few times, I've fallen asleep lying in the bathtub and waked up miserably shriveled and cold. Once I woke to find my daughter asleep in the bathroom with me, her pillow on the cold tile floor.

When I was the age my daughter is now, they couldn't get

me out of the bathtub once I was swishing the water up and down, making hairdos on a head piled with suds, or carving the soap into a bracelet—or into a boat to carry me away. My mother and everyone would be knocking on the door, telling me to get out—but never coming in, as though afraid of what they might see if they did. I would dawdle and dawdle for I don't know how long. Now I don't play and dawdle, or think about men. I don't even worry about our lives—my daughter's and mine. I just sit. I sit and observe the formation of stains on the shower curtain, observe the way my legs look different when they are under the water as opposed to when they are out. I put them under. I take them out. The shape of them looks different. The color of them looks different. Everything about my legs looks different one way from another way. It is so amazing to me.

I let some more hot water in, lean my head back, hear the closing theme of *Outer Limits*.

I'm flying. I'm high—up in the air—far up away from the trees, from the bushes, the people, the cars, the apartments. I can move with my arms and be lifted—I can fly in the air like I'm swimming! I am whizzing along! I am zooming along! I can hear the S fluttering on my chest. I can see our place. I can see our window! The woman down there, the woman behind the glass, can she see me? Can that woman see me flying? Hear me singing?

Why can't my mother hear me sing? Q

DON DELILLO

The Rapture of the Athlete Assumed into Heaven

TENNIS PLAYER, a man in his early twenties
INTERVIEWER, an older man or woman

The TENNIS PLAYER, *all in white, falls to his knees at the moment of triumph—head thrown back, eyes closed, arms raised, one fist clenched, the racket in the other hand. He is frozen in this pose, his body glowing in strong light, with darkness all around.*

At the sound of the INTERVIEWER's *voice, the* TENNIS PLAYER *begins to rotate as if on an axis, completing a single 360-degree turn in the course of the play.*

The INTERVIEWER *carries a hand mike and walks out of the darkness about five seconds after he begins speaking. He circles the* TENNIS PLAYER, *moving in the opposite direction, stopping occasionally, making as many revolutions as the monologue allows.*

INTERVIEWER: How special it must feel, Bobby, finishing off a career in this fashion, it must feel like a culmination you could only dream of years ago, growing up without a role model, without a high school on a hill, using a borrowed racket that smelled of someone else, it must feel like a vindication, an affirmation, winning the big one at last, the one that's eluded you all these years and in all these ways until today, playing before the Queen, the King, the Jack, the Ace, growing up without a blond girl in a Buick, without a girl with long and tawny legs who rocks beside you on the porch swing, coming from behind to win the match they said you'd never win, the doubters and skeptics, the pundits, the clever little men with bad bodies, how sweet it must be to reach your goal at last, so many disappointments, so much sorrow, growing up without sideburns or a personal savior, totally missing the point of rock and roll, undersized and out of breath but determined to pre-

6

vail, it must feel like a restoration, an eternalization, growing up without a mom in flat-heeled shoes, finding a racket in the bracken and taking it to bed, obsessed, depressed, a boy without a girl in a blue Buick, how transforming it must feel, a blond girl with a tawny body slightly shiny in the moon, answering your critics at last, the nay-sayers and doom-sayers, the gloom purveyors, the nihilists and realists, playing before the Queen Mother, the Gay Father, the Battered Wives, tell us quickly how it feels, growing up without a junior year abroad, so many failures, so much sadness, we're desperately eager to hear, it must feel like a permutation, a concatenation, growing up without a girl in a tawny field, a sunlit blonde in a summer dress who lets you put your hand, who lets you touch, who says shyly in the night, growing up without an old covered bridge nearby, how super it must feel to achieve your biggest thrill as an athlete on the last day of your life, to know the perfection of the body even as your skin loses heat and energy and hair and nails, and now we're all enfolded in your arms, you are the culture that contains us, we're running out of time, so tell us quickly, time is short, tell us now.

The INTERVIEWER *fades into shadow before he finishes speaking.*
The TENNIS PLAYER *completes his rotation.*
He remains motionless in intense white light for five seconds.
Black. **Q**

PATRICIA LEAR

Hot

I will get older and wear wool suits and count on myself, and the baby will ride around Wall Street on a motorcycle. But for now, here is how it barely is—enough things to sit on my soul and bring me down to a soft whirring, to stop my hair from whipping and slapping me in the face—some things, not myself, to count on.

Sweet darling, I am hot by morning, when the sun edges the drawn shade in gold and I wake to the clacking and the chimes. There are dried-stiff fish skeletons you might comb your hair with layered out there, out my window, layered like bananas in a bunch on palm-tree trunks, and they are what I hear clacking most like plastic in these dry days. There are wind chimes out there too, mixing in, and the fellows downstairs run their dryer mornings; I can smell their softener gusting up here, and it is a comfort.

For now, it is all too beautiful sometimes, with me having so much wide grinning time, a desert of time, a triple feature of time—time it takes courage to have.

I rub my finger, I wet it first and rub it along the ledge, moving slow, bulldozing stuff up into a little hill, shaping it, squaring the corners with my fingernail, working to get it right. I know when it is right.

With their long leaves, those trees paddle the air, slapping and grating themselves up along my screen, grating their raggedy ends clear through, and snowing down to the other side into my room, screen-powdered to dust along the ledge.

I write "my little baby" in the dust. He is bucking on the floor, his diapers barely hooked on his hipbones, the floor probably no cleaner than the ledge, and I take hours to do anything, years to do anything, with breaks only for food, for bath, for naps, but I have all day most days, me up on the bed

8

eating candies I keep hidden, maybe under my pillow, so the baby will not know; I take care to keep the papers quiet, him up here with me, or on the floor on his little woven blanket, and me sneaking a piece of walnut fudge I buy on our walks. These days will not go on forever.

There is a house being built. Sawing out there, which is a nice thing, a nice sound, though I admit I need the wind chimes, would never be without them now that I know what they are about. You should get some and hang them on a porch. No, don't—I might give you some—oh God, and listen to this, here is the thing: in bed in the dark. That, and then me in the middle of all these things, my favorite things outside and in here. I love slipping my body down along the sheets themselves. One that I know, there is one who knows me and tells me things, me in a moonlight that turns us sand-colored slick with sweat, our ribs rippled dunes, the moon squinting at us from behind that aforementioned fishboned tree out there, projecting jungle patterns neck to thigh. What comes is all the reasons anyone would ever want, or could ask, for waltzing on with this life.

I leave the baby with Rosa days that I have to, and I leave him at the ritzy church when there is a ladies' luncheon, a function for me to weasel my way out in the world from. I kiss him goodbye on his cheek—he is my moon child, I could eat him with a fork, eat him with a spoon, and I leave him safe in the church ladies' good care. I leave him finally, regretfully, dragging my netted soul out the door and away, like when he screams in the night and I have nothing else in me that I can see to do for him—which breaks my heart. And it is at those times I find I have to shut the door and go on and do something else.

Trembling with freedom, I tear my name tag off, seek out shadows, glide along walls, hug myself up in the carved-stone alcoves of this church that smells sweet with simple chicken salad and warm breads, those Parker House rolls, like the gusty dryer downstairs—and chicken salad, or did I say that?— and something else, something in the wood or in the hymn books, something they light and burn. I slide out the back way into a bucket of afternoon stars dumped over my head, goofy now (it's that freedom), and I do a pratfall for old Will sitting out there after he has done the cooking, but before he does the dishes. There is Will settled nicely into loud daylight— which, like flashbulbs in the face, is painful, would be even for an old-time movie queen, *ta dah.*

Will can be counted on to smile. He smiles, and wears one funny shoe for his poor hurt foot that—I do not know why— never heals, it is an open sore. Something from tending the yard. I kneel in front of him, I bow my head, I do not know why I do this either, but I want to see, and I slip the open shoe off his foot and pick up the folded gauze.

Does not bother me in the least. It has nothing to do with me, me with fingers wet with saliva tracing the curve of waist, slipping along over this body with the crazy trees out the window and the music of the wind chimes and the little baby bucking up on his knees in his crib, little fat knees to chest, in one movement grabbing up his bottle and rolling over on his back, and me in my bed with the other slipping me up onto him, pulling me up by holding me and tugging under my arms.

I sit side by side with Will on the bench I move him to, him hobbling along close beside me, the bench in a softly shaded archway with the vines and climbing roses weaving through, as, my loose skirt slipping low between my legs, I comb my hair out from where I have it twisted up, high and wound around with a patterned scarf. Then I twist it back up again off my neck, just the same way I had it before.

Will puts one splayed hand on my knee, pushing up, and he says, Miss, you too young for this place, which always makes me cry for some reason whenever anyone says that to me, and I stop with my hair and tip my face so sun splashes, glancing off my face, and I let him move his hand, and for a while, I do not flinch.

. . /.

I cross the street, then another street, and then wander down, winding like a vine where things get stylish to my husband's office, where I look up and find his mirrored windows. He said he saw me once down there on the sidewalk, he said, with a soft Santa Ana stirring my hair so some strands stuck to my lips, and the ends, he said, the ends, they danced up like flames.

Sometimes I keep going down the street to try on narrow black dresses, or to look for shoes with straps that buckle across the instep, or to sip Cokes with lime slices and ask for crusty lemon sole with slivered almonds at my husband's little brick building of a town club, me sitting off alone in the dark paneled dining room.

And sometimes I go into the building where he has his office, and I ride up in the elevator to his floor, and walk down past his gold-lettered door straight to the office across the hall, not my husband's office, but another office where there are receptionists safely corraled off, walls of files, doors somewhere that open quietly and close quietly. And bouncy music, that grocery-store music, that dentist-office music, lively but muted. There is, too, the sound of butcher-block paper tearing off a roll in the back. I find myself a seat with the others, and like them, I look at magazines, or stare at the fish tank, or look up at the people occasionally walking by outside in the hall.

Of course he sees me, he knows me, and almost with a ballet step, he turns a quarter turn, his hair longer and slightly sawtoothing over his collar as he tilts his head and muffles his smile. Now, of us women who wait, I have been the quietest one, the littlest mouse sitting in the big leather chairs, and he says my name before I begin to rise to my feet, never looking at the others, never knowing if they know he has taken me out of turn, and I follow him back through his little maze of halls, out the back door, down to the underground garage where his car is parked, not far from the church where my baby is with the church ladies, and we get in the back, and he reaches up my skirt, and he pulls my panties down, or sometimes just moves the crotch aside with his hand, and I help him, I hold it to the side for him—he is not a magician—as I lie back on a leather seat smelling like leather.

I wander alone the streets of this place; it is afternoon quiet, hushed before rush hour, and I know I have to get my baby early, before the other luncheon ladies come for their babies and questions are raised.

The church babysitting lady is so kind and my baby happy and clean. I take him to the park, he is awake and ready, and we sit off alone near a fountain of water that falls like ropes, and to the sight of this I nurse him, the milk ready in me for him, and I nurse him.

From where we sit, I know I could see the windows of my husband's office, and next to them the others, if I looked. I do not know what the wife my husband had before me did to him that made him leave her, and now me, to make him leave me, but now I do know that, no matter what it was, sweet baby, I would do it, too.

The baby tugs at my breast and works his face into a frown, he works so hard at his nursing. He is so small, his back square and flat, it fits the palm of my hand, though everywhere else he is round but his back. It makes me straighten my back up with him as I sit and look out at the cars going by. They seem to pull the asphalt up in strings, it is that hot. **Q**

The Beast, Watered

"Dan?" she said.

"Yes?" said Harry.

"What're you doing?" said the girl.

"Putting on my shoes," Harry said.

"God," said the girl. "What time is it?"

"Don't know," said Harry. "Two. Maybe three."

The girl raised herself up on her elbow. He saw her watching him as he buttoned his shirt. He saw her hair hanging down all on one side.

"God," she said, and blinked.

He got his shirt tucked in. He stood with his arms hanging at his sides, considering, then bent down to the girl and put his face next to hers. He lifted her hair up into his face. He rubbed her hair against his face. He breathed the girl's hair up into his face. The girl made a sound. He felt the bed heat of the girl from underneath the covers.

"Got to go," he said.

"Okay," said the girl. "Dan?" she said.

"Yes?" said Harry.

"You'll call me?" she said.

"Sure, you bet," said Harry. "First chance I get."

He walked fast, crossing the tracks, crossing the bridge, trying to get things going. His breath came out in big clouds. His teeth chattered. He hunched his shoulders and kept walking. Along one full block of shop windows he watched himself walk. At the end of the block he turned, went past three doors, and then went into Ryan's.

"Hey, Harry!" said the bartender. "What's shakin?"

"Plenty," said Harry.

He winked and rubbed his hands together. The bartender grinned and shook his head.

"Coors?" said the bartender.

"Nope," said Harry. "Not tonight. Think I better have some of that whiskey you got."

"Comin up," said the bartender.

"And a pack of something," said Harry. "I don't know—something menthol. And matches."

The bartender screwed up his eyes as he poured the Seagram's.

"You don't smoke, do you?" he said.

"Not much," said Harry.

The bartender came over with the cigarettes and Harry took a ten-dollar bill and a keno ticket from his wallet. On the back of the keno ticket there was a telephone number written. Harry studied the curves of the writing. He lit a cigarette. He saw himself in the bar mirror lighting the cigarette. He held the cigarette near his chest and the smoke curled around his shoulder and past the side of his head. He tried a smile in the mirror. But did not like what he saw there. He crumpled the keno ticket in his palm. Then he held the cigarette down near his knees, watching the smoke split itself around his leg. He kept moving the cigarette to different parts of his body, first with this hand, then with that hand, to his lap, to his neck, his face. He did not let go of the keno ticket. He watched himself.

"Hey, Harry," said the bartender, "gonna smoke that thing or not?"

Harry looked at the bartender. He crushed out the cigarette in the ashtray.

"Guess not," he said.

"I don't know about you," said the bartender.

Harry filled his mouth with the whiskey and puffed out his cheeks, rinsing. He moved his tongue over his teeth. Then he put his nose to his shoulders and his arms. He pulled his shirtfront up to his nose. He raised his knee to his nose. He checked once more in the mirror, then collected his change, left a tip, and kept the keno ticket.

He took his shoes off in the hall and turned the key to the door. The latch clicked. He held his breath, pushed through the door, then closed it quietly behind him. He had nearly made it to the bathroom.

"Harry, honey? That you?"

He stood where he was.

"Yeah," he said. His voice sounded funny to him. "It's me," he said.

"God," said the woman. "What time is it?"

"I don't know. One, two." He hated his voice. "Not sure."

He emptied his pockets, keeping the keno ticket in his hand, and started taking off his clothes outside the bathroom.

"What've you been doing?" said the woman.

"Oh, you know. Ryan's."

He moved just outside the bedroom door. He could see her in there, propped on her elbow.

"Coming to bed?" she said.

"No," he said. "Not unless you want to sleep with a saloon. Think I'll get a shower. Pretty smoky in that place. Check these."

He tossed his trousers and his shirt onto the bed and turned to go to the bathroom.

In the bathroom, he took one more look at himself, then squeezed the keno ticket into a tiny ball. He got on his knees and dug through the bag under the sink. He dug through tampons, through disposable razors, through hair, and through wads of Kleenex before sticking the keno ticket down at the bottom.

He shaved twice.

He urinated—and he noticed the smell!

It smelled to him as if he had been eating something

funny. He stood there at the toilet awhile before flushing it.

He turned on the shower and got the water very hot, and waited in front of the mirror until the glass fogged. He stepped into the shower, bent his neck, and let the water wash down over his head. He tried not to think—not about the funny smell or about the keno ticket or the cigarettes or the girl's hair. He let the water wash down over his head until he no longer needed to try not to think. Then he raised his head and let the water hit him in the chest.

He got out of the shower. But he did not get a towel. Instead, he dropped to his knees, pulled the bag from under the sink again, and began going through the tampons, the hair, the Kleenex, the shit. He felt his heart beating. His ears filled with his heart beating. He dumped the bag on the floor and spread the stuff out, his eyes moving over everything, his fingers testing everything. He tried to remember the girl's face. He tried to remember her voice. He tried to remember anything she said or what she had felt like when he had felt her. But there was only the funny smell.

He kept pawing on his knees. **Q**

The Orphan

We're two different boys, no blood in common, with only one set of parents: his. Mine are out there somewhere, of course, but they move too fast to be of much help now that I need help constantly. After my junior year of college, once they were sure I'd graduate, my parents sold their house and land and left on a never-ending vacation. It started with a double tour of Europe—first the Great Churches, then the Great Food—and picked up steam when they got to Orlando and bought a option-packed RV, thirty feet long, with cruise control and dual antennas that rise up like missiles when Dad thumbs a button under the dash. Now there's no telling where they'll end up. According to my uncle, who keeps track, they live in the campgrounds of national parks.

This is a growing trend, I hear: seniors on the road. I saw a graph in *Newsweek*.

Kyle's parents are here to stay, though. They're people to count on, solid, and all you need for proof of that is one good look at their kitchen. All their major appliances, and the Markhams own them all—from microwave oven to ice-dispensing fridge—are set in flush with the cabinets, as units, not like at my old house in the country, where everything ran off extension cords and looked as if it might be gone the next day, tilted up onto a dolly and wheeled outside for the annual yard sale. My parents bought things used and sold them wrecked; Kyle's parents buy new and send in the guarantee card.

The night I first set foot inside their house, the Markhams welcomed me into their family. Kyle and I had gone there for dinner because the apartment we'd rented that week still didn't have its gas turned on. We'd been out of college only a month.

"We see this house as a resource now," Mrs. Markham

told me after dinner, settling back in her chair. "Richard, don't you agree," she asked her husband, "that Kyle and Wade, if they're smart, will view our house as a resource?"

"That's correct," Mr. Markham said. He wiped his mouth and put down his napkin and folded his hands on the table. "You see, Wade, it's not like when I was young. Everyone needs a network now."

"I'm getting ice cream," Kyle said. He pushed back his chair and stood up.

"Honey, please, we thought we might talk now. All of us. Together," Mrs. Markham said.

"Go ahead. But I need ice cream," Kyle said.

Kyle's parents watched him leave the room. Their heads moved slowly, like videocams, then slowly scanned back to me.

"So, Wade, you're a farmer," Mr. Markham said.

I said, "My father was a farmer, yes."

"That's what Richard meant," Mrs. Markham said. "That farming's your background."

"Your heritage," Mr. Markham said.

"Got that," I said.

No one talked for a moment—it hit me that I'd been curt. I tried a joke: I said, "If getting up at five in the morning and skidding around on frozen manure is what you'd call a heritage!"

I saw Mr. Markham frown. I saw his chin form little dimples, like a golf ball. He said, "You shouldn't dismiss your upbringing, Wade—I envy that attachment to the land. I'm sure our Kyle would have thrived on such work."

Kyle came up beside the table and stood there with his dish of ice cream, eating. I hated ice cream and Kyle knew it—that's why he hadn't brought me any. His mother accused him of rudeness, though, and instead of explaining the truth of the matter, which would have been simple enough, he told her I was on a diet.

She gave me a look of apology. Mrs. Markham said, "You should have warned me, I would have served fish. We're on a diet, too, Wade. Tell him, Richard, explain the program. Explain our longevity diet." I saw Kyle standing behind his mother, grinning. One thing he'd always said about his folks was that they had plans to outlive him.

"I'm glad we had the veal," I said. "The veal was delicious, really. Thank you. Thanks for everything."

"No problem," Kyle said. "Hey, Mom, you know all those game hens in the freezer?"

"Kyle, sit down," his father said.

Kyle patted his stomach. "Too full. Could Wade and I maybe take those game hens? Our freezer's totally empty."

His mother shrugged.

"Thanks," Kyle said. "Well, Wade, you ready?" He sucked his spoon, then set it in the dish. "I'd like to get back for *Monday Night Football*," Kyle said.

"Why not watch it here?" his mother said. "Wouldn't you rather see the game in color, Wade? On a great big Magnavox wide-screen? *I* would." She smiled—I couldn't believe her teeth: a perfect set so straight and white she could have worn them as charms on a bracelet.

Kyle said, "Sorry, Mom, Wade has to work."

Kyle looked at me, winking.

I looked away.

I wanted to stay.

I liked those big TVs.

Two months later, in August, the car I'd been driving to work—a junker Chevy my uncle had sold me for twice what he would have gotten from a stranger—ground to a smoking halt on the freeway and had to be abandoned on the shoulder. I didn't know what to do. I panicked. Kyle didn't have a car to lend me, my office was not on a bus line, and purchasing a replacement car was simply out of the question. Ideally, I would have had money saved—I drew a decent paycheck—but something about being out on my own, a full, free participant in the booming local economy, had blown away my thrifty instincts. It wasn't rent or utilities that killed me, it was the little things: quality socks in every color, imported beer, designer frames for my glasses. Stupid things. The worst one was a certain kind of candy bar, Swiss, with triangular segments, dark and chewy, which I had tasted just once as a kid because they didn't stock them in the country; but now, in St. Paul, those candy bars were everywhere, calling out to me, dragging me down, making me eat at least ten of them a week at over a dollar-fifty apiece.

The day after the breakdown, I called in sick to work and stayed home with Kyle, watching TV. For lunch we had a cheese tortellini salad, a gift from Mrs. Markham. Anyway, it made me vomit, and so Kyle took me outside for a walk, saying I needed air.

"Tell you what we'll do," he said. "We'll use my Visa to rent you a car. Pay me back whenever."

"That's forty bucks a day, Kyle. That's ridiculous."

"Then we'll just borrow my dad's car. Relax."

"What if one of your interviews pans out and you need a car for yourself?"

He reached into a pocket for something. He looked depressed.

"I didn't mean to cast doubt," I said.

He shucked off the film from his new pack of Camels, the same brand I'd started him out on in college and then had had to give up myself when I saw the effect they were having on someone else.

Kyle said, "I never actually made it to those interviews. I should have told you, I saw this doctor." He blew out a perfectly circular smoke ring and poked it with his finger. "You know how I've felt so tired lately, really incredibly tired? So anyway, they tested my blood, Wade, and I'm sick. I've got mono."

He tapped off his ash in his palm and blew it into the street like a kiss.

"Mono," I said. "Didn't you have that already?"

Kyle said, "Not this form of it, this is new. It started in California last year and now it's practically nationwide. They call it the 'Screenwriter's Syndrome,' or something, because it strikes the educated, mainly. No way I can take a job now. Really sucks, huh?"

I told him it certainly did suck and asked him to wait on the sidewalk while I ducked into a deli.

I couldn't help it.

I bought a Toblerone.

"About the car thing, that's easy," Kyle said when I came back outside. "My folks can buy you a car. They'd love to. I'll just say it's for both of us."

He pounded his chest and coughed experimentally, hoping, I suppose, that something solid would come up. "My folks are crazy about you," he said.

He coughed again and finally got up some mucus, I think.

More important than mileage or styling, Mr. Markham told me, the thing to consider with cars was *safety*. We were standing in a rainy Honda lot, waiting to be noticed by a salesman. Kyle had gone to the office for water to wash down his antibiotics. Ten minutes later and still no salesman, Mr. Markham delivered a speech about the decline of good service. He blamed it on an erosion of values but didn't get specific. Thinking it was my fault that we were there at all, I asked him if we should leave; he shook his head. He'd brought along a paperback book that rated the major compacts according to their performance in crash tests. He was paging through it, finding the model he wanted.

"This is our baby, the two-door Prelude." He showed me the rain-spotted photograph. "In theory, I'd prefer to buy American, but Detroit's so far behind these days in inner-frame construction—" He saw something over my shoulder.

"Kyle, get back in there! It's wet out here, you're sick!"

I turned around. I saw Kyle throw up his hands and do a fancy pivot, mock ballet.

His father closed the book and looked at me. "You kids don't share razors, I hope. Toothbrushes? Because you don't want to catch this virus, Wade. Bad enough that it went after Kyle. These modern bugs, they don't play favorites."

We found the right car without assistance, the only new Prelude left on the lot. We opened the doors—they weren't locked—and climbed in. I sat in the driver's seat, hands on my lap, too embarrassed to take the wheel. When Kyle had mentioned the car to his parents, he'd said that if we didn't get one soon, I would have to leave our apartment and live all alone across town, where my job was. Leaning back in his chair, arms crossed, Kyle's father had considered this, then made his judgment: "That's simply not an option, Wade, splitting you two kids up. You're far too good for each other."

Mrs. Markham had agreed. "We all need backup."

Mr. Markham was patting the gearshift, his wedding ring clicking on the plastic knob. "You any good with a manual, Wade? Ever use one?"

"Yes, I have," I said.

"Because if you haven't," Mr. Markham said, "an automatic's safer. That's what Rachel and I have in the Volvo."

"Either one," I said. "Whatever. It really depends on what Kyle likes."

Mr. Markham plugged in his shoulder strap, rocking forward to gauge its play. "My son is not a driver, Wade—he didn't grow up on a tractor like you did. I don't want him taking this car out alone."

It took me a second to hear the command in this. "Fine. Okay," I said. "Trust me," I said. "He won't."

Boom, boom, boom—it happened that fast. First I received a ten percent raise; then, one week later, my boss took me into his office and fired me. He didn't give me any reason.

I never found out why I lost my job, and the mystery of it opened a hole beneath my feet—it sent me into a long mental wobble that made it hard to for me to get up in the mornings and look for new work. Kyle's reaction only made things worse. Instead of giving me sympathy, he tried to recruit me into a club—the lonely rebels, the poets, the shafted—which I would not have minded being part of if Kyle had not been its president.

My consumption of fancy candy bars tripled.

I'd had it with Kyle by then and he knew it. I'd had it with driving his father's car. I'd spent the winter plotting my escape, a traitor at the Markhams' Sunday dinners, smiling as I chewed their food, but staring straight through them with X-ray vision.

But I was more dependent than ever.

After a week of watching my face break out in snow-capped pimples and letting my fingernails grow, I told Mr. Markham about what had happened. He warned me not to blame myself.

He said, "Take Kyle, for example, this virus. Ever since he caught this bug, I've asked him to take things easy and not get all down and blue that he can't be more productive just now. You see, Wade, with you always working so hard, it made my son feel guilty, understandably so. But what he soon learned— and what you're learning now—is that bad breaks happen. They do. As a farmer, you should know that. Would you blame yourself for a grasshopper plague?"

"Probably not," I said.

"Of course you wouldn't," Mr. Markham said.

We were sitting on his sectional sofa, watching the Twins lose to Oakland on the big-screen Magnavox. Kyle had fallen asleep in an armchair, not because of his "mono" but because he'd been drinking beer all afternoon. That's what he did with his days—drank beer and played with his stereo, copying albums onto tapes.

I dozed off on the spongy sofa and woke up the next morning under a down-filled quilt. Someone had taken off my shoes. I spread my hands on the puffy quilt and watched them slowly sink, pushing out the air. I turned on the TV by remote control and flipped between cartoons. I wandered into the kitchen, opened the fridge, guzzled some orange juice straight from the carton. When I turned around to throw out the empty carton, I saw some plastic-wrapped melon next to a bowl of granola. Tucked under the bowl was a note.

"Enjoy your breakfast, tea is in the pot. Gone to the mall with Kyle to buy you kids an IBM PC."

A computer.

I didn't remember asking for one.

I finished my second breakfast, took a piss, and then, for no other reason than that I had the run of the house, I went upstairs with my cup of tea to see the Markhams' bedroom.

I'd never seen it before. It was gigantic. I sat on the bed and looked around.

I thought of my parents chugging through Yellowstone, driving from geyser to geyser, happy, pointing out wildlife to each other.

Working for Mr. Markham was not like working at all. The pay was good, the hours part-time, and for Kyle there was the added advantage of never having to leave the apartment. The computer sat in our living room next to Kyle's stereo and was linked by a modem to Mr. Markham's office in Edina. All that the job involved was inputting names and addresses obtained from various sources and collating them into specialized mailing lists: owners of pure-bred dogs, say, or Iowans with boats. Then you snugged the phone in the modem, entered a secret password on the keyboard, and sent the lists back to Edina.

It didn't upset me that Mr. Markham had never formally asked permission to make our apartment part of his office. What he'd done was install the computer, and then he'd suggested a few days later that if we wanted to, we could use the machine to earn some money.

The great thing was that the presence of all that technology gave us a reason to keep the place clean. Kyle's fatigue tailed off. He didn't look particularly good, but he said he felt good, and he worked even harder than I did. Myself, I got bored at the terminal, the desk chair hurt my butt, and I couldn't stay at it for more than three hours a day; but Kyle, who'd always loved electronics, could sit there nonstop, testing new functions, playing games, typing away with his headphones on, absorbed. He joined a "computer pals" network that let him trade programs and personal stories with people nationwide. Sometimes he stayed up till three in the morning "talking" with a Korean girl in Boise. Kim was a high-school senior whose parents were very poor, Kyle said, yet they'd spent over three thousand dollars to buy her a machine and give her an edge in science and math.

A month went by, then two, then three. I dropped my idea about moving out and finding a place of my own. I bought a cat with Kyle and fed it every day. And when Mr. Markham's birthday rolled around, I switched on the screen and plugged in the modem and sent him an electronic greeting: "Your faithful employee, Wade."

We were out in the car, just driving and talking, laughing about something, when Kyle started to cough. The cough sounded to me like a bad one, deep and stringy. Kyle turned his head and raised his hand to shield me from the droplets.

I asked him if he was all right.

"I doubt it. This mono has cycles." He inhaled and his chest was full of whistles. "Not that anyone gives a shit."

I didn't know what to say to that.

He stared out the windshield. His jaw was set. "I was okay when I had those pills, but now, as an experiment, my mom and dad say not to take them."

He coughed again, bending all the way forward. "I got those pills on *prescription*! You saw the bottle—I had a *prescription*!"

I could see he was getting himself worked up now.

And then the blood came up. I was reaching for the shift knob, thinking that I should find a store where Kyle could get an aspirin or something, when suddenly I saw blood on my sleeve—fat red threads of it, like loose yarn. I couldn't take my eyes off the blood. At first I didn't know whose blood it was—I thought maybe we'd been in accident. It was crazy. I checked the road to see if we were still on it. I looked at my sleeve again—then I looked at Kyle.

His head was tipped back against the seat and his hands were on his knees. A long twist of blood was hanging down from his mouth. The blood didn't drip, it swung.

I shifted down and took the next exit. I knew the route by heart. My goal was to get there before they ate dinner.

I wanted the Markhams to see all this blood on me.

And then I wanted to live there. **Q**

He Has Been to Macy's

So he went on down there. He went there in his truck. It rained.

Mrs. Finn was in the kitchen, kneading dough for her daily bread. Around her waist was a calico apron the mice had long since chewed through.

The last stretch, he walked, leaving his truck, with the rain coming in, at the edge of a vast cornfield. He had a sideways way of walking, the hind foot some way sluggish, likely to drag or skip. He was wearing a brown fedora, a linen jacket, a pair of just-shined shoes. He had shot two holes in the floor of his truck so the rain would run on through.

Flour bloomed from the top of the counter and clung to the skin of her arms. Hens laid eggs in the outhouse. It was a bad day for making bread.

He came through the tomato field, picking his way between the knocked-down stakes and the brown plants now bent over, a tangle where there were once neat rows.

Birds clung to the eaves of Mrs. Finn's house. The screen was missing from the big kitchen window. Onward he came, passing beneath the shelter of the big live oak, that great swooning creature of a tree whose limbs kissed the banks of the river. Some Yankee, Mrs. Finn surmised.

The man knocked at the frame of the front screen door and received no answer. He had come too far for this. He would burn her out if need be. He knocked at the door again. Crocodiles fed on the banks of the pond. Something big swept down from the big live oak and beat the air above his head. Then came footsteps, such soft things, slippered feet on a bare wood floor.

But Mrs. Finn did not open the door. She watched the stranger through the fly-specked screen, her fingertips pressing against it. In this screen there was a tear, torn by the wind that tore through here she could not remember how long ago. She cleared her throat before she spoke, leaned toward the man, pressing against the screen so hard that the skin of all ten of her fingertips bumped up through the grid.

"That's pneumonia weather," she said.

She pointed outside with her chin.

The man's tongue came out and, curling up, caught drops that fell from the fedora's brim. The tear in the screen tore toward both ends of Mrs. Finn's body.

"Leave them things on the porch now and come on in where it's dry."

The man's tongue was curled up into a ditch that the rain dropped into and ran down through. He stood there. He would catch her, too. He could see Mrs. Finn was going to dive through that screen, hands wide like that, leaning toward him, pointing her sharp chin.

Mrs. Finn cleared her throat again. She eased back, said nothing. Dustings of flour left on the screen showed where her fingers had been.

"Amend me," the man said. "I had thought your eyes blue," the man said.

He was sitting cross-legged on the bare wood floor, tapping his chin with his finger. Mrs. Finn's hands were in her lap. Her eyes were as bright as the eyes of a bird, but only the whites were blue—a pale blue, like the moon when it blues in a certain season.

"You are wondering why I have come," the man said. "What there is I can tell you."

There was a parrot on the screened-in porch poking at the man's wet shoes. *Buenos días*, it sang, *Howdy do*.

The man said, "I could tell it suchwise, missus—from Coney Island to my house."

He took a sip from the cup of tea Mrs. Finn had made for him. The parrot climbed into one shoe.

"It was dusk," he said, "one wintry, one-color day. Where it was I had come back from, I can no longer recall. I had come in my usual way, expecting, as usual, no one. But there he sat on the steps of my house."

They could hear palm fronds clash beyond the missing screen of the big kitchen window. The smell of bread traveled the rooms.

"George had been out to Coney Island," the man said, "where Atlantia overtakes the land. There he swore the sky had swelled up above him. 'I lay on my back on the dirty sand and the sky came and laid down along me,' George swore, 'heavier than a woman and pleasanter, too, until I thought she would . . .'

"Ah," the man said. "You have your doubts. You have your doubts, I see that."

Mrs. Finn had pulled to the edge of her easy chair. She was fingering the hole in her apron.

"George assured me you would not, in the beginning, understand. Try to understand," the man said. "I present it to you as a single tale from Coney Island to my house. But George had been all over. He was a thoughtful man. George thought, 'Inside me is the Kingdom of Heaven.'

"But even heaven scared George then. The bones of the roller coaster sang in the wind. Fish washed onto the dirty sand and rolled back into Atlantia again. 'Would heaven be like *this*?' George feared '—this rancid, tumorous gray?' If this was how, after all, he looked inside, would this be his share of the Kingdom of Heaven?

"He said, 'Waves breaking easy on the dirty sand made a dim, high-slapping sound, like a great deck of cards being shuffled.'

"George palmed his chest, where the swelling was. 'How about,' he joked, 'a bit more color: cholera-green, pneumonia-blue, salmonella-yellow?' "

Mrs. Finn crossed her legs at the ankles. From the ditch her apron made of the space between her legs, both of her hands were lifted, pressed between the man's two hands like the pages of a book he might read. The man knelt up. How pale his face was. Mrs. Finn felt herself being prayed to, though it made no sense to her why. The man kissed the tips of her fingers.

"Listen, little bird. A small sleep," he said, "a small slumber, and the memory of him is me."

The man's hands slipped so softly from hers that Mrs. Finn's hands were left praying.

The rain let up; the house grew quiet. A crocodile slid into the pond.

The man sat back on his haunches and, hearing the hard weight of him against the bare wood floor, Mrs. Finn brought her knees together, and she stood, and sure that she was not watching him, instead the man listened, such soft things, those footsteps, going away and gone now and coming back again.

When Mrs. Finn came back into the room, the man was in George's easy chair, the one chair in the one room the wind had not walked through, picking and choosing from among their things. Mrs. Finn sat down on the floor on the cushion she had brought to the room for the man to sit on. The man poured the last of the tea, though it had gotten cold by then, into a cup Mrs. Finn drank from.

"Suppose this," he began again. "Reckon that when the Beginning began Our Father exploded. Our Father art tiny trillions of pieces riding above the world.

"His was a strange pilgrimage," the man said, "your George's was. He caught the next train for Manhattan. George thought, 'If I believe in one God and that God exploded, does it not stand to reason, then, that in the Beginning there was one man—one set of eyes and arms and legs, one heart, one head—and that he, too, exploded?'

"Suppose that the world is a single body where each man's pain is every man's sorrow, where each man, created in a shattered God's image, jettisoned into the stratosphere by the force of a huge explosion, came falling upon the earth.

"That makes so many ways of fitting together, and only so many pieces."

The man leaned toward Mrs. Finn, bending away from the back of the chair, the joints of his hips creaking.

"See my hands," he said. "Look here."

Mrs. Finn held his hands in both of her hands. She turned and turned them over. "And these, too," the man said, leaning ever more, his eyes so close to Mrs. Finn's eyes that their eyelashes were almost touching.

"These are your husband's eyes," he whispered. "I know all about you, duckie. I have been all over."

Mrs. Finn lit a candle between them. The last of the sun had gone from the sky and left, not the crimson of frequent evenings, but a fat, dank, ineluctable gray, noticed not by Mrs. Finn nor by Mrs. Finn's stranger, talking on as they did in small ways, strangers now to outside things, talking against the silence that pressed against their lives.

The stranger lowered himself from the easy chair and sat bent-kneed beside Mrs. Finn on the bare wood floor.

At the edge of the pond, in a halm of reeds, a cat stalked dragonflies, beetles.

Again the man spoke, and again, though he himself seemed not aware of it, a change usurped his voice.

"I have been where George has been, only not so far, not quite so far as George is now, but elsewhere, yes, all over. I have been to Macy's," said the stranger, rocking now so fast on his haunches that Mrs. Finn put her hand on his arm, desperate to calm him.

"I know all that George knows, more and less," he said. "How things cost you an arm and a leg, catch your eye, spin your head. I know about fathers who say to you, 'Son, I couldn't do without you, you know you're my right-arm man.'

"But, duckie? When George's father died out, George himself kept walking."

The man raised his hand to his upbent knee, lowered his mouth to Mrs. Finn's hand still calm against his arm. With his teeth, he tugged at her wedding ring. With his tongue, he parted her fingers.

"There is a man near Macy's," he said, "who sells plastic birds for a dollar. His one sleeve hangs empty. 'Hey, mister! When you fill 'em with water, they sing!'

"This got George thinking. His head swam with thoughts. If you lost an arm, was George's way of thinking, if you had to do without, then was there not some way, if you one day decided you could not keep on doing without, to go ahead and find your man and get your arm right back again? Was your arm not a body walking, stopping at storefronts, selling things on the corners of streets? Or if not, was it maybe a body still falling, a body you would find in the Kingdom of Heaven, in a place where, finally sorted through, everybody looked like you?

"When your own body betrays you, parts of you keep living with living people's bodies: for the people who are whole, there are parts of you left. There is a web of the parts of you left that the people you love will know about.

"Do you see now why I have come?"

The stranger carried the bird into the kitchen and filled it at the kitchen sink. Hens were coming out of the outhouse, white beyond the palm fronds, beyond the missing window screen, just shapes as far as the man could see, not seeing the twist and tilt of their heads as they heard him, blowing through that bird a cock's crow, and Mrs. Finn heard the man crow, too, her head, too, atilt, perched again in George's easy chair, and then the *coo* that was like the coo of a dove that the parrot on the porch failed to parrot, giving off something more of a *caw* and, Mercy, Mrs. Finn thought, this with what was now so mercilessly the crunkling of a crane in the kitchen, and the parrot failed at this as well, calling out *coo* instead, the parrot calling *coo coo ricoo*.

The cat trod circles on the screened-in porch.

The man squatted, set the bird beside Mrs. Finn on the arm of her easy chair. The weight of his heart he gave her, also of his head, his forehead resting against her knees. She had her sister's knees he knew. His breath passed between them.

" 'My heart,' he said, 'has gone out of it. My heart, I can tell you, is my Martha running through a door of glass. You must understand why I've come,' George said. He took off his hat and his linen jacket and he set aside his shoes."

The man slipped off Mrs. Finn's slippers. He rolled down Mrs. Finn's knee-high stockings and pulled them past her feet.

" 'Please,' he said. 'Give Martha my love.'

"He loved you very much, you know. He sent me with his love," said the man.

The bird let out a broken scream, its plastic tail caught between Mrs. Finn's lips, though her legs, like two wings, parted.

The man circled her cheek with his nose, tongued her ear, her tiny mouth. She bit him.

"Are ye living in the shadder of the cross?" she whispered.

She could smell George's smell on his clothes.

"Shadder of the cross," the man whispered.

"Shadder of the cross," he said. **Q**

Soil

I have a son, he's eleven. I killed a man one time, in Hadleyville. Those are the only things that keep running through my head. I tell my son he lives in this: the yard where his grandfather used to cut wood, Georgia black soil and masonry, things remembered and spent—some his—hard and disquieting, and the people—some of them ours—dispossessed, patient, a foreshadowing—

I love the smell of wood just after it's been cut.

My name's Atwater. I work in a place near Atlanta. It's soft stuff—ag research and government contracts—and my supervisor's a good guy—retired army, a sergeant—so I don't mind it. Sometimes I work Saturdays and bring my boy with me. He wears a lab coat and plays on my computer. I was in a dugout canoe near Cixzqua—part of the black Amazon—when he was born. I had a grant and was working down there. I had no idea his mother was pregnant. She was a biochemist from Rochester—I didn't know her very well—and she worked in our lab only for a month or so. When I got home, my mom had the baby. She had a room for him all made up.

Sometimes I watch my son walk to school. He doesn't see me. I follow him until he meets up with his friends. Then I turn around and go back home.

I got drafted right after I left Emory. They put me in Special Forces, but they ship me to California when they find out I'm a soil and botany specialist. I spend two years killing plants from the Mekong delta. I start listening to Mussorgsky. There's this captain there named Ehrlander, a Mussorgsky and wine freak. "We don't exist in the army," he says. "We tarry, we dwell, we hang on, and nobody knows we're here."

Ehrlander has a girlfriend named Janice in Santa Rosa. They take me into Napa Valley sometimes. It's nice, the three of us in Janice's convertible, listening to *Boris Godunov*. It's the first time I've ever been out of the South.

It was all different then.

When my hitch is up, Ehrlander and Janice take me to this wine auction. They buy a two-hundred-fifty-dollar bottle of wine. On the way back home, we get drunk on some gin.

I'm coming home from work. I'm going to see Bobby. Bobby and me went to school together. He tried to enlist, but he had a disk that wasn't in the right place so they didn't take him. He lives with this black girl named Lana in Routon. It's quite a way from the highway and he's the only white guy in the whole place. He doesn't do much of anything. He wanted to be a poet, but he told me once that he just got too tired. We played baseball together when we were growing up.

When Lana sees me, she squeals. She likes me. Bobby comes out.

"Hey," he says. He is wearing shorts and a white dress shirt.

"Don't you have a tie to go with that?" I ask him.

He smiles. "You look good," he tells me.

We go inside his place. It's run-down and there are no steps into the house. He gets me an iced tea.

"When are you going to start being a drunk?" he asks.

"When're you going to be a poet?" I ask.

"I don't know America well enough yet," he says. Lana comes and sits on his lap. "Me and Tocqueville. Still got a lot to see."

"When are you going to come over to the house? We can play some ball," I say.

"Your kid's too good for me to play with. Bring him here. Squalor builds character."

He asks me about guys we grew up with, his brothers and sisters, his parents. "I see no one," I tell him.

"So many names," Lana says.

I finish my tea. Bobby and me go outside. Lana waves. Bobby starts to say something. His voice won't come. We stand around for a few minutes, hands in our pockets.

"Hey," Bobby says finally.

"What?" I say. He looks sad and I turn my head away. I look at Lana.

"Sometimes it gets real cold out here," he says.

Sometimes I go to the library and look at the pages of books. I like dedications, epigraphs, all that stuff.

I'm playing catch with my son. He has a good arm. It's cool, but the sun stings the back of my neck. My son throws from a quick, short windup. The ball pops when it hits my glove. I feel old and think of Bobby for a minute.

It's February, years before now. I'm standing in the warehouse where I work. I'm ordering some things for the lab.

"You like musicals?" this guy asks me.

"They're okay," I say.

"I love them," he says. "The dancers. Astaire, Kelly. The girls especially."

He's a big guy, huge hands, really pale. He has an army jacket and cap on.

"You work here?" he says.

"In the lab, yeah," I say.

"Why don't you get me a job?" he says.

"Geophysics, chemistry. That's where I work."

He shrugs his shoulders. "I was in Korea. Marines. You in the service?"

"Yeah," I say.

"Nam?" he asks.

"California," I say.

I'm going home. I stop in Hadleyville to get gas. I'm

leaning over my windshield, wiping it off, when I see something in the glass. I turn around and see the big Marine coming after me with a tire iron. I duck and he catches me in the shoulder. It hurts like hell at first, but then my arm goes numb and I don't feel it. With my other arm, I go for a throat shot. I can tell he's in real trouble the minute I hit him. When the police come, I can't tell them much. I don't know his name, where he was from, what he was thinking about. Maybe about a warehouse job, some bar in Panmunjom, Cyd Charisse.

One night I was listening to Mussorgsky at my folks' place. It's a nice night. My boy is a baby and I still have my jarhead cut. I sit and watch my boy sleep, the scent of cedar and unreal quiet the only things outside. I suddenly have this feeling. I can't talk. I want to call my dad. I get my boy and pick him up. I sit down with him in Mom's old chair.

I hold him. We just sit. **Q**

Mothers

1 THETIS

The ancient Greeks were greatly concerned with armor. After mighty Achilles was done in by Paris, the poets tell us in great detail how Ajax and wily Odysseus saved his body from the Trojans. But it was his armor they both were interested in, and Ais slew a herd of sheep in his rage at being denied the prize; then, in shame, slew himself.

Thetis, no doubt, was more interested in the body of her son, but the poets tell us nothing of this. They do not tell us how she wept in relief that he was gone, relief that at last she was freed from the world of men.

She had been unlucky in her men, unlucky in love. Lover, husband, son—she had wanted none of them, suffered them all.

"Thetis! Thetis!" Zeus had moaned, dry-humping her in the dark shadows of a portico one spring evening on Olympus, his big ham-hands digging into her tender girl's buttocks. "Meet me on Samos—cave—southeast corner—tomorrow—noonish—ahh!"

Hera found out about it, sent old prissy busybody Prometheus with the tale that Thetis would bear a child greater than his father—one of the most hackneyed ruses on the books but guaranteed to have some effect on Zeus, who was touchy on the subject of patricide. So he agreed to marry Thetis off to Peleus.

Peleus! He spent most of their wedding day vomiting up the fine wine that he drank too much of, undiluted. He had to stand on Hermes' helmet to kiss her—even though she was small for a goddess—and his breath smelled of garlic—garlic! which to Thetis was decaying vegetable matter, natural corruption, humanity, mortality, death.

She slept with him only once—that was the deal with Hera.

After that once, Zeus wouldn't want her anymore, Hera knew, nor would any god.

Peleus came to her on their wedding night, his little thing dangling like a pale fig that had grown in the shade. She sighed and lay back, opened her legs. Except for the smell of garlic and stale wine, she would hardly have known he was there. A night breeze wafted through the window. She closed her eyes and imagined great Zeus coming to her as a bull, a swan, a shower of gold. Before Peleus had finished, she was asleep.

She awoke at false dawn—Peleus snoring beside her, his cheek and neck wet with spittle—and wept, not because she was married to a dying man, a mortal, a pitiful thing who could not even throw a good woman in a wrestling match, but because she realized that the true curse of her marriage was yet to come: a son, whom she would not want but would love and pity and grieve for even before his death.

Half-god they would say of Achilles, the mortals, in awe and envy, even though one could no more be a man-god than one could be a virgin mother. To be a mother, you had to suffer the man on you, in you, suffer *garlic*—and to be a man, you must suffer death.

She wanted her son to live forever, dipped him in the river Styx, botched the job, thereafter lived in fear.

He was the butt of jokes. At the age of four, he whipped the bully on the block, then ground his heel on a cocklebur and ran to his mama screaming as the boys howled in delight. She took him onto her lap, stroked his head, just as she did years later when Agamemnon took his Briseis. He was a grown man then, but slow-witted, easily confused by Agamemnon's arrogance, old Nestor's pleas for moderation, Athena's sudden appearance in his tent. He ran to his mama.

For a great, hulking brute, he wept easily. History tells us of three times when mighty Achilles wept. He wept at the loss of Briseis, who might, in a different fate, have become his wife, Thetis' daughter-in-law. He wept once more, crawled up into his mother's lap and wept, when his buddy Patroclus was killed by boasting Hector, and he wept when old King Priam knelt before him and conjured up a vision of fathers and sons.

Peleus! That's whom Achilles wept for. His *father*. Old garlic-reeking Peleus, who mounted the goddess Thetis one dark night and rutted with his pitiful little dying thing, moving her no more than a puff of air, as the gods of Olympus snickered into their goblets of gold. Achilles finally became a man, we say—we are to admire him most, we say, when he remembered his *father*.

Thetis could have torn her hair.

But that was not her curse. Her curse was to suffer a man on her, then to watch her little boy die on the dusty plains of Troy, to see him weep the fourth time, which history does not record: when the arrow pierced his heel. He wept for the old reason—he did not want to die any more than Hector had, who ran around the walls of Troy three times to escape his fate, or Patroclus, wearing Achilles' old armor, or Agamemnon, home from the war, with a robe thrown over him as his wife stabbed him once, twice, thrice.

Neither Homer in the *Iliad* nor Virgil in his *Aeneid,* nor any of the minor poets, tell us what Achilles felt when he was dying. They had turned their attention to something more interesting: armor. Homer devotes one hundred and forty-five lines to the great shield alone.

Of Thetis, after the death of her son, the ancients tell us nothing at all.

2 MARY

Once, at a wedding in Cana, when there was no wine, I went to him, my son, and I said, "We have no wine," and he said to me, his mother, "Woman, what have I to do with thee?" His *mother* he said this to. I could have wept.

What have *I* to do with *thee*, I should have said. I should have told him about the wind that came in the night and pushed me, blind in the darkness, onto my back, pushed my legs apart, my robes up around my ears, almost suffocating me—a groping, rude, nasty wind. That wind would not take no for an answer.

The word become the wind become the Word, one of them, one of *his* friends said later—Luke, I think it was, the brainy one, or maybe my nephew John, when one of his fits was on him, his eyes rolling back into his head. I never could understand what they were getting at, all nonsense to me the way they'd talk, Jesus the worst of the lot. He was always a mystery to me.

"Woman, what have I to do with thee?"

The idea of it! If he could have felt that wind, I tell you, he would have known something then! Pushing an innocent girl's legs open that way. I'll never get over it.

If it'd been Gabriel, now, an angel of a man . . . He was making the rounds then, first to Elizabeth, then to me. "Blessed art thou among women," he said, one of the oldest lines. And God help me, it might have worked—his hair shone so in the brightening air!—if it'd been he who came in the night. But no. It was a *wind,* I tell you, a cold lover.

I had been popular, all the boys liked me, I could have made a good match, but after the wind came, what could I do? Joseph. Only a fool would take me in my condition, and that meant Joseph. Stuttering, stammering, clumsy Joseph, who all the children teased, stole his eggs, dropped goat turds in his milk, set fire to the thatch roof of his woodshed. After the shining man Gabriel, how could I let that great klutz put his calloused mitts on me? "I'll marry you, Joseph, but you must promise never to touch me. I'm the child-bride of the Lord."

I grew to pity him, but never to love. It was Jesus I loved from the first. What a bright, gentle lad! He was never a bit of trouble, always minded his mother, would bring me a wild rose when they were blooming by the river, or a bit of honeycomb. How I'd weep when he ran to me with his nose all bloodied by the village bullies. He would never hit back, he was too gentle for that.

We doted on one another. That's why I couldn't believe

it when he said that thing to me: "Woman, what have I to do with thee?"

It was the rabbis, I guess. They filled him with ideas too big for his sweet little head. I remember once when he was seven, eight, the rabbi caught him in the temple pretending to read the Torah—as if a poor carpenter's son could read!—and kicked him on the backside so hard that he had to sleep on his stomach. I was furious. "Joseph, go give that rabbi a smack he won't soon forget!" I said, but the big cow only mumbled into his beard and did nothing. "It's all right, Mama," Jesus said, always willing to forgive.

But I don't think he ever quite forgave. When he threw that fit in the temple many years later, I think with every kick he gave those oxen and sheep, with every money changer's table he sent flying, he was remembering the boot of that rabbi.

By then I had lost him. He'd started into that son-of-God business—I'll take my share of the blame for that—and I knew it was only a matter of time until they would have enough on him.

He was never strong, and he lasted only three hours on the cross. I thank the Lord for that. Still, what a thing for a mother to witness . . .

Mothers should not outlive their sons. I didn't want to, I prayed to God to let me die before my son, I swear I did, but prayers are not meant to be answered. If my prayers had been answered, it would have been Gabriel who came to me that night, and not *wind*.

So Jesus was gone and I was left with Joseph. Sometimes I'd think I'd go insane how he'd go for days on end without saying so much as a word. But it wasn't easy for him either, I know. He never touched me. Only once, when he was old, he came to me, the need scarring his face like an awl, and begged me to lie with him. "Stand there," I said, positioning him at arm's length. "Now, if you can blow me onto my back, blow my robes up, and force my legs apart with your breath alone,

I'll let you do what you want." How that man blew! I laughed until the tears ran down my cheeks.

Thinking back, though, I feel sorry for all of us—Jesus, Joseph, and me. It's a hard life. Thank God, it doesn't last forever.

3 MOTHER

She had never felt such a wind, she said, as the one that almost killed her the night before her eightieth birthday. There had been a tornado watch out all day, and the warning sirens went off as she sat down to dinner. She had her own basement, but she did not want to die alone, so she headed across the street to the Smiths'. There wasn't a breath of air when she came out of the house, but before she was halfway across the street, the rain fell like a great river turned on end. Then the wind hit just as she was trying to cross the rain-gorged ditch left by a gas-main repair crew. She couldn't get up out of the ditch and would have died there if Mr. Smith hadn't run out into the storm and pulled her to safety.

How she laughed about it afterward!—but I could tell it had frightened her. Once the bravest of women, she's frightened often now.

Her eightieth birthday has hit her hard. Seventy had not been bad, she had handled seventy, and sixty was a breeze. She worked forty-four hours a week at sixty—she could do forty-four hours a week standing on her head!—had her own teeth at sixty, and Uncle Arthur (arthritis) hadn't begun to pay his visits yet. Fifty? Why, she couldn't even remember fifty, it'd been that easy, a snap. Forty, though, that'd been the hard one. "I thought I was finished at forty," she'd tell us over and over again. What "finished" meant she never said, because a mother can't mention certain things to her children, but it is easy enough to figure out.

She had had enough of us—children—by then anyway. We had all been a surprise, she told my wife once, we were all unexpected. Her last pregnancy came when she was thirty-seven. She thought it was a tumor. I would like to think that she was grateful to find that it was me, and not death, growing in her. But one can't be sure. She has always been an independent woman, and perhaps she thought of each of us as a violation and an encumbrance.

By her fortieth birthday I would have been walking, talking, and potty-trained, and she would be finished with conceiving. "Get a job. Work just long enough to pay off the new car," my father pleaded. So she went to work and abandoned me, howling and clinging to her skirt, with Mrs. Pierce.

The new car was a loathsome gray 1950 Pontiac. The earliest nightmare that I can recall is of my mother in that Pontiac driving up to Mrs. Pierce's house to fetch me. Slowly, slowly, it rolls down the drive, then magically overturns. My mother stares up at me, eyes open, dead.

The dream is easy enough to interpret: parental abandonment, etc., etc. But I don't think I was as resentful as the dream would seem to indicate. I was afraid of *everything* as a child, and the nightmare was just one more howling demon among the thousand that haunted me.

I was more resentful years later, perhaps, when she left me with Mrs. Burton—months and months—as I recovered from rheumatic fever. Mrs. Burton popped her gum and watched soap operas hours on end as I lay on the bed, paralyzed with hatred and boredom. I began to read. Classic Comics were my favorites, and my first Classic was the *Iliad.* Since I had not read the original, I would hardly have missed Thetis, who is not mentioned in the Classic *Iliad.* But I was moved by great Achilles' tears as he thought of his father, old Peleus.

My father was big as God. With one of his great fingers he'd lift me into the air. We were inseparable; as we walked side by side, I'd run four steps to match his one, long, slow stride. I'd find dark, dry places for him to hide his cigarettes— from *her.* Mother was our common enemy. She seemed to be always in a rage against him. It took me years to realize that it was rage born of fear. We were both afraid for him.

My father was dying all my life. His first heart attack came when I was three. My mother would have been forty then. "I thought I was finished at forty," she'd say. My sister and I would think of Jack Benny and laugh, but it was no joke to her. *What* was finished? Some things can't be contemplated by a son: my father, big as a bull, snorting in lust or stalled in impotence over . . . No no. Some things cannot be contemplated by a son.

She was always in a rage at his foolhardy ways: he would not cut back at work, would not lose weight, insisted on hauling the old chifforobe out to the back yard and trying to break it up himself instead of letting me do it, as Mother ordered. "What kind of man they must think I am," he wheezed, rubbing his left arm and eyeing the neighbors' kitchen windows as he surrendered the ax to me.

He chewed garlic—read in an article it was good for the health, he said, but it was really to hide the odor of cigarettes on his breath. At some point—when I was eleven, perhaps, or twelve—I stopped helping him hide his Chesterfields and began helping her find them. It was not betrayal. I was growing more and more afraid for him, and I began to understand, if not share, my mother's rage at his heedlessness.

He was afraid, too. He would lie in bed at night taking his pulse, she said, taking it over and over until she would want to scream. It maddened her that a man could fear so much for his life while he ignored his immortal soul. He had stopped going to church, you see.

By then my faith was suspect, too, although I still went to church out of habit. I liked the hymns at least, especially at Christmas time. A Nativity scene would be set before the altar. Fat, lugubrious tears would begin to well when I gazed at baby Jesus in the manger. What a fate he was born for, I would cluck sadly. I didn't think of Mary. If I prayed in those days, I would pray for my father to live forever. I did not pray for my mother.

He did not live forever. It was the third heart attack—a bright, cold Sunday morning—that killed him. The night before, trying to make conversation with an indifferent son, he had picked up one of my textbooks and said, "This looks interesting." I shrugged. "It's just a book on mythology."

More and more, I took refuge in books; I especially loved the ancient poets. They have a way of coming at the hard things indirectly, spinning good yarns out of what must have been private pain: Homer longing to see his father's face; Aristophanes' son dead at Syracuse; Aeschylus and his jealous wife. But, I wonder now, what do we learn from them, really? Through suffering, wisdom? The suffering I understand, but where in my forty years is the wisdom?

Yes, forty has hit me hard, too. Sometimes I think I'm finished at forty.

She was not quite sixty when my father died. She'd had a lifetime to prepare for it, and she took it well. She worked forty-four hours a week, plus overtime. Sixty had been a breeze for her, and at seventy she still mowed her own yard and shoveled the snow out of her driveway. But now she's eighty, failing, and afraid.

What have I learned to help her die?

I would remind her of her brave deeds. Remember how as a girl, fleet-footed as Atalanta, you would run down the horses in the winter woods and ride them, laughing, bareback. Do you remember how you beat the flames on your sister's burning dress—with your bare hands, still scarred—and then ran into the woods when the doctor came to change Bernice's dressings? You ran and ran, hoping to outrun her screams, but they always found you, and you would run back and touch her, gently, someplace where she had not been burned. Do you remember when you and Daddy walked across a barely frozen river one Sunday? Just to get to the other side, for no other reason—you were just young and in love and foolhardy and wanted to get to the other side.

I live in another state now and visit my mother three times a year, at Thanksgiving, New Year's, and once in the summer. When we leave after each visit, she will stand in the driveway and wave as we drive down the block to the corner, turn and drive on until we disappear beyond the Wallaces' house. She will stand there waving goodbye in the wind, rain, snow. I've given up telling her to go back inside. She's superstitious, obviously, and thinks that waving us on our way will ensure a safe journey. Obviously, she still worries about me. I'm past forty now, have high blood pressure, smoke, don't watch my diet. Probably she's afraid that she'll outlive me. It occurs to me that this is what she's been afraid of all along. **Q**

Dancing for Men

The boy is on the coffee table. He is saying, "Daddy, watch me two-step!"

His mother is in the kitchen pouring reconstituted milk from the jug to the bottle.

The boy's grandfather flew in World War I. He flew a biplane the color of engines. He dipped and swooped and often thought of home, of his generous cows. He thought of his wife. How would she fill the silo? He got a bullet in the throat and came home to farm.

Tonight he is coming for dinner, and the boy is in his underwear dancing for his father.

Now the boy is dancing for Grandpa, too, while the women ladle gravy in another room. Grandpa is wheezing through that hole of his.

"Boy, do you know the turkey church trot?" Grandpa asks.

"No, sir." The boy stops dancing. His underwear is as clean and white as teeth.

Grandpa dances the turkey church trot.

"Come here, boy. I've got a secret," Grandpa says.

The boy's father is on the couch. He is reading *Field and Stream.*

Grandpa has his lips against the boy's ear.

"Do you know why I've come home?" Grandpa asks.

The boy says, "No."

"Mama missed me."

Grandpa is whispering. It's as if he's taken the boy's ear into his mouth and bitten. **Q**

Gadamer's Maid

Gadamer's maid was large. She kneaded bread with her large hands, rolling it, pulling it into braids, plumping it into flour-crusted loaves. She would carry Gadamer's grandchildren from the entryway to the playroom, resting their heads on the taut lumps of her biceps. Her hair was like an animal's. In it one could smell the rose hips she took with her to the bath, and what a sturdy bath it must have been to have supported such a woman, virtually iron, with thick-ankled legs.

The house was hers.

Gadamer, in his study, was just a small man among books.

This maid had a rusted bicycle that she steered to town on Thursdays. Gadamer had found it rusting at a garage sale and had walked it home to her, for the maid was made to carry the groceries for such a great distance. Once she had the bicycle, she balanced herself on the seat and leaned into the air like a pilot. The *Metzger*'s meat was fresh and it would be wrapped in swatches of broadcloth. She piled everything—bags of fruit, canned goods, starched linen, kitty litter, everything—onto the seat and pushed the bicycle back through the streets of Heidelberg, back to Gadamer and the tick-ticks of his typewriter.

There were pomegranates then, too, that later, in Brussels, would be hard to come by. Gadamer had become quite fond of the fruit during an early lecture tour in the Singhalese schools of Burma. He pried off the seeds in bunches of three or four and picked at them with his fingers. He would examine the fruit on the high terrace of his house, then wave the cracked pomegranate at the maid, and she would join him. Every afternoon it was the same, the maid standing, waiting for Gadamer's invitation.

Socrates was a German.

Gadamer's maid used dialectics to twist her bread.

She sang lieder.

She knew Schumann's granddaughter, poor cuckold.

Years passed without interruption. Christmases with canned hams and apples, and a month of Good Fridays slipped away.

The trouble began when an impetuous student called from the States. Al Lingis had referred him. Levinas had given away the telephone number. At Penn State they sit in bars and talk Gadamer, Gadamer.

"Is Gadamer home?" the student asked.

He was making the international connection from a telephone outside the bar.

The maid grabbed a towel on the way to the bathroom and wrapped Gadamer in a terry-cloth robe. But the caller had been disconnected.

"It was from the United States," she said.

Gadamer nodded, his face all wet and red. There was nothing he could say. Telephone calls from the United States were rare and the connections often poor.

This same student finally came to the door. He said, "I've come to interview Gadamer."

How could Gadamer have known? How could Gadamer have been ready?

"It's just an interview," the student said. "I have a recorder and some tape." He had been running, it appeared. His eyes were tight and his hair hung like sweaty dreadlocks on the long stretch of his neck.

Gadamer and the student sat on the terrace.

German afternoons are lovely.

The furniture was Etruscan.

"You are an awful man," Gadamer finally said when the day was done and the crows had come to pick at the pomegranates. "These questions have been discussed for too long.

Where is your heart? Everything you say, even the truth, will come out like a lie."

"I've traveled so far, Gadamer," the student said.

Gadamer's knees were shot, and even the bulky cane he carried with him could not support him anymore. When he walked, his body twisted away from the direction he was headed in. Indeed, he needed his maid to hold him and to guide him. He stood at the side of the table, supporting himself, and talked into the student's face. "I am still a man, and you are not so strong," Gadamer said, whipping his cane across the student's head and pushing him off the terrace into the pond of goldfish.

That was Gadamer's last afternoon in Heidelberg.

By the time the student came to, Gadamer's maid had packed their bags and they were on the train to Brussels.

They buy a villa.

Gadamer has begun to annotate. The maid can hear it going on, like a small fire in the house, wherever she chooses to stand.

"When shall we visit America?" the maid asks.

"Never," Gadamer says.

Gadamer's maid laughs, holding the sides of her apron like a sheet.

Lengths of damask are sold in town, wrapped tightly around themselves—flower prints, burgundy pistils, bulbed orange stamens, forest green, pine green, royal blue—and piled like commodities on the tables. Gadamer's maid pulls the material through her machine, pumping the foot pedal and bunching and pulling until there is a dress. She wants to find a husband among these men of Brussels, a man with thick arms and tattoos all over them.

In January, Hannah Arendt comes to stay, the old Jew descending like Mary Poppins. Her suitcases are wooden and she wants a bedroom of her own. She arrives sometime past midnight, dragging her cases along with her in the dark, for the cabby has run back off through the streets of Brussels, leaving the visitor to greet the colossal maid alone.

"Hannah!" the maid says, and holds out her hands.

"It has been some time, no?" Hannah Arendt says.

"You should have written," the maid says.

"How is Gadamer?" Hannah Arendt says.

"He is an old man," the maid says. "He wants to spend his time annotating, but he really doesn't have the strength."

"This is why I have come," says Hannah Arendt.

The light from the porch makes Arendt's hair look lighter than the pictures you have seen of her on the flyleaves of her books, almost white, and the skin on her hands is as thin as onion flesh.

Oh, that Hannah Arendt!

There is nothing but clothes in her cases, not even a pencil in her purse. Her handbag is filled with tubes of lipstick and those peppermints she has learned to suck on after eating and during conversation. She ties the candy wrappers into bows and leaves them hidden in the crannies of your couch or under your Holbein, Lotto, or Salor Turkmen Oriental rug. Arendt's recklessness, her disregard for the tidy and kempt, keeps her one step ahead of Gadamer's maid. She is the cosmetics queen. If she had not aged so indelicately, Lancôme would have pasted her face in every Nordstrom's in America. But she has given it all up—books, ontology, typesetting, ink.

Yes, she fills up the house with her fancy odors. But Gadamer sees and smells nothing. Gadamer is going blind, and the tight vent of his trachea is closing in like a tin heat duct in March.

"Did you happen to bring any fruit?" Gadamer asks.

He has the hard red pomegranates in mind, but he also misses cherries and the fleshy apricots.

"Fruit? No. Customs and all that," Hannah says.

She is busy folding away his pages of typescript, slipping them into her purse while Gadamer looks off the terrace.

"Then a peppermint maybe," Gadamer says. His lips are thick and wild.

Hannah is cool. "Nope."

You must know that Gadamer's maid is made jealous by all this, for it is clear to the maid that Hannah keeps her hair well frosted, spends dollars on her Greenwich Village coiffures, whereas the maid's hair is straight and German. My God, the maid has left everything in Heidelberg, her red bicycle and her house!

"Oh, it's all a story," Hannah says. "Heidegger never loved me in the curtain folds of the lecture hall." She lifts her purse with the stolen chapters, tightening the clasp.

Gadamer is looking out over the trees. He can see monkeys hanging in the branches and troops bivouacking in the distance.

He will never walk again.

The next morning, before Gadamer has finished his bath, the maid departs for New York.

"Tell Gado I'll miss him," the maid says to Ms. Arendt.

New York is well lit, and the maid is introduced to many men. She is driven from street to street. She dances. She takes up smoking.

She is forty-three and no dummy. **Q**

Sin, Sin

"The girl tells me hounds won't get her legs open tonight," Mary Todd says. Chet is setting his bowling bag in the closet, next to the umbrellas and his hockey stick. He bowls in the afternoon leagues at the Bowl-a-Rama.

Celeste is on the couch with her hands between her knees. She will hear what the man has to say and hold her position. She will not comb her hair, not put on underpants. Celeste just watches.

"The girl bluffs. She is telling stories. The girl has so many stories. All day she 'laxes on the couch and puts these stories together," Mary Todd says.

"Are you sick?" Chet asks Celeste.

Celeste shakes her head.

"Tired?" Chet asks.

Celeste nods. She has the will of a Buick, the staunch of a Chevrolet.

"She will not speak. She will not speak," Mary Todd says. "The girl plays mute." Mary Todd has risen from the chair where she watches her game shows. She has loved Alex Trebek in this chair. She has beat the buzzer on *Jeopardy*.

"Cancel the arrangements," Chet says.

"Then it's double duty tomorrow night," Mary Todd says. Words fall from this woman's mouth like chunks of candy, pieces of Formica. She turns to *Wheel of Fortune* and guesses at anagrams.

"Do we understand each other here?" Chet is saying. "Do we have an agreement?"

"I have the list here in my purse," Mary Todd says. "I have the list here. Here are the names. Here are the addresses. I will expect to be reimbursed."

"Is this a game of imbursements? Is this what we are doing here? Because I didn't know it, not until this very minute, when I just heard those words of yours. Where are we, now that we have come so far, for you to sit before me and speak of imbursements?" Chet doesn't know what to do. "The imbursement, the payoff that will be ours, the what we are in this for, is financial security in our old age," Chet says.

"Birdshit!" says Mary Todd.

She has squared off in front of the television set.

Chet says, "Birdshit? Birdshit? Where are we when a wife learns words from the television, when she uses those same words to talk to her husband? Where are we then? What have we become?"

Chet is a little man. Mary Todd outdoes him by two inches and sixty-three pounds. He could not move her from where she is if he tried. He could not wedge his foot against the sofa and jerk her away from her game shows. But his rhetoric is powerful. It renders Mary Todd useless.

Celeste does not tabulate the ins and outs of her captors' arguments. They kidnapped her months before. She has grown weary of keeping score. She lies on the couch and thinks of Sammy Hagar. She wants his cock inside her. She knows it's big. She had front-row seats at the US Festival.

Chet says, "Are we all right here? Are we all settled?"

Celeste says, "Why don't we change the channel? Why don't we watch a movie?"

The wind in Barstow comes right up to the mobile homes and does not leave. It moves like determined gypsies into the crannies of aluminum siding. It comes in the heat, auspicious, full of warnings for this and that, and it never leaves. Mary Todd can hear it as she watches her game shows. She sits in her chair and it speaks to her.

For Celeste, it is the wind of her fortune.

All day long, these women sit in the mobile home, the windows locked, the door locked, the locks locked. They watch television while the mobile home leans to the plateaus, then back again to the flat stretch of desert.

Celeste tells the same story to every man. She wants to make filthy videos. She stands on the floor and grabs herself. "I want the camera lens right here. However," she said to Jack Scofield one night, motioning with her hands to the aluminum of his mobile home, "this is not what I envisioned."

"You have talent, acting ability," Jack said to her. "I could spot it when you came in the door. She is a real fine actress, I said to myself. I said to myself that maybe you were in Barstow because you were making a film, maybe one of those French films you hear so much about. Honest to God, this is the truth. I said these words to myself."

"Look at this," Celeste said. She lay on the floor of his trailer, her skirt hiked up over her hips. Only when Jack started doing her did she breathe again. "That was my death scene," Celeste said.

Jack said, "I thought you were dead. I really did."

One time, Celeste stole Mary Todd's camera and took a roll of film, picture after picture of herself. She got in close. She snapped and snapped. "I'm on my way there," she said to herself.

Legally, Chet kidnapped Celeste when he found her hitchhiking home from the US Festival. Celeste knows this will lead to something big. This is a step in the right direction.

Celeste is from Spokane.

Lives are riddled with sin.

For her birthday, Chet buys Celeste an exercise kit. It is a bag of rubber tubing with handles and pulleys.

"The man at the Bowl-a-Rama says isometrics is a law you can live by," Chet says.

Celeste is on her back, with her feet and hands in the equipment. She pushes one way and then another.

"Is there an instruction book to the thing?" Mary Todd asks. She has turned away from *Wheel of Fortune* to watch Celeste exercise.

"It's very simple. No instructions needed," Chet says. "The man says nothing can go wrong. With isometrics, sprained ankles are a thing of the past. They also told me it also cures cancer."

Vanna is turning letters on the television, filling in the missing clues to all the puzzles.

"And did the man say if this particular piece of equipment removed fat, trimmed the waistline, or toned muscles?" Mary Todd asks.

"All of the above," Chet says. "Besides, I don't see the point in delineating all the functions. If everything these cords could do was written in an instruction booklet, it would have to list all the cancers."

"Will she overpower us now?" Mary Todd asks.

"What is power with a tool like this?" Chet says. "The word becomes meaningless."

Celeste exercises every day. Mary Todd becomes more guarded. She turns down the volume on her shows and watches Celeste exercise.

The man Celeste loves has a Super 8 camera. His name is Delbert Simmons. He rents her twice a week and they make filthy movies. Celeste becomes different women.

"My Marie, my little Antoinette," Delbert says. "Do me the favor of looking to your right. Open your mouth. There. Oh, yes!"

Celeste plays Nefertiti against the great desert backdrop of Barstow. Dressed in robes, Nefertiti consults necromancers.

"One god, the sun god, you say?" Celeste says, stroking her chin.

Chet begins dating with fervor. Women from the Bowl-a-Rama, from the Albertsons, from the Barstow Foundation for Women's Studies, fill his tiny mobile home, and Celeste, relieved of her nightly trips from trailer to trailer, must receive them all. She cooks omelettes, filling them with broccoli and avocados. She finds pictures of Brighton Beach at the flea market and hangs them on the walls. With yards of cloth and a handful of tacks she reupholsters the old cum-stained couch.

"Where did you get the girl?" Miss Winscomb asks. "Such marvelous help is impossible to find in this part of the world. Such delicacies she treats us with. Such a delicate girl."

"Oh, yes," says Miss Strapworth, "she is a treat, a veritable treasure to have around the house."

"Celeste has been with us . . . ," Chet says, resplendent in brown tweed and a pair of burgundy loafers.

In the early morning, when the plateaus and mesas are still dark, Chet walks through his mobile home. He pauses by the couch where Celeste is sleeping and goes outside where Mary Todd is waiting for him. A thousand stars are falling through the air, a meteor shower of great proportions. He can see the masses of other mobile homes sitting in the darkness, the stars above them splashing like milk over Los Angeles. **Q**

The Bouncers

Two men, mesomorphs, sat on either side of a red door. One was me, Lance Beety. It was an outrage to me, that name. I think, for a while, it propelled me out of myself, allowed me to think and act differently. What could my parents have been thinking of, though? These were quiet Iowans; the heritage was of stolidity in the face of soil; "Lance" in no way fit. The other door-watcher was a friend of mine, Jim Burl, "Milton" to any passing wit. Jim was educated many years beyond me, an easygoing brain who'd published a small thin book I'd never seen. Just before the time I'm thinking of, he'd been let go from a position with an Ivy League university. It was an entry-level deal out of the math department, and they'd decided not to keep him on. At loose ends, he was of course having trouble at home. I had been installing at first carpets and then phone systems. There had also been a stint as a server of subpoenas and a coder of documents. Nothing had hung together for me. Which is why, in precis, Jim and I were where we were.

On the other side of the red door, two streets intersected. One followed the river while the other bent downtown. The numbers on the door looked as if they'd been applied with a house-painting brush. A sign (also hand-lettered, but more neatly), said 500 CLUB . . . OUR MUSIC THIS WEEK . . . followed by the days of the week and the band of the day.

Jim and I had been lounging and vaguely expiating since his return from New York, frequenting sports bars and a road next to one of the runways at the airport. We happened into the 500 one night and the manager surprised us by being someone we knew from the old days. Our spastic conversation was concluded by an offer of employment.

"I already have a large black person to handle the assholes, but I grow weary of sitting by the door checking IDs. Does five dollars an hour sound fair? Please say yes. The rough stuff is at a minimum these days. It's cyclical. You want to die in a knife fight, you have to go to Palmer's, I think. We can go for months without an incident of *any* sort. Our music, for one thing, is folkier than it used to be, and the place is turning into a college bar. I regret the ambience shift, but the nonviolence dividends are real. The age went down and then it went back up and we get a lot of youngsters in here. The rule is, card everybody. You get a guy who's thirty-two and he's outraged, tell him to shut up *right away* and give you an ID. I want this place to have something of a reputation. You know what I mean. A no-nonsense kind of place. You can get lit but not necessarily have to watch your step every inch of the way. Passable music, fancy beer if you want. You know."

We signed on.

First night, a baptism of fire. An asshole came in and ordered this outlandish series of mixed drinks and liqueurs. He leered at the bartender and let his jacket hang open to reveal a holstered weapon of indeterminate caliber. The bartender, Gary, said something demurring and the asshole leapt away from the bar, holding his jacket wide open. *"I want the drinks and in the order I ordered them! I just got laid off and I'll take everybody with me into the afterlife if I don't get the drinks I ordered in the order I ordered them!"*

Our large black man ("Beaver") rolled the guy into a little squealing ball and I put in a call to the police.

Then nothing for a month.

It was a Tuesday, midnight, one degree below zero. Vehicular traffic was sparse through the intersection, and pedestrian traffic nil. The band was called FYI. They performed (according to their manager, whom we were shortly to meet, a guy who routinely altered people's lives) a kind of feedback-augmented neo-Muzak.

FYI finished their last set, loosened their ties, and lined up at the bar. The manager (his name was Derf, Derf Greelis) came over and said we were off the clock, so we lined up, too. We drank two shots in silence and let a philosophical pensiveness build.

Jim said, "There are signs we don't get. Do you believe that to be true?"

"Surely."

"In nature. It's speaking to us all the time, right? 'The earth he heard had made a noise but it was no sound he knew, no language spoken . . . more a harsh shadow than a sound . . . a single note of retreat.' That's William Eastlake. Language and information are everywhere. In the air, in the soil—the Universe itself is in some sense raw information. You know what I mean? And we don't get it. Ninety-nine percent of it: it flies right through us. Even if we *hear* something, even if we *sense vaguely* that we're being *spoken* to . . ." Jim was making little quote marks with his fingers every other word, up and down and up and down. ". . . Even if we stop and wonder uneasily for a second, we're bound to think what's happening is that we're *forgetting something we were supposed to do.* You know what I—? We go blank and then fall into a daydream or start *worrying aimlessly.* I was walking along this trail in the woods, along the edge of a gorge, last summer in New York. Very idyllic. A narrow strip of woods flanking a steep gorge, a stream, a waterfall . . . It's early in the morning, I've read the *Times,* had my coffee, the water is flowing, the birds are chirping—*I'm whistling a merry tune.* Life is good. I'm on my way to *work.* I'm *working,* it's *steady,* there's *hope for the future.* I take a dogleg in the path, and there on a tree stump, right at the edge of the path, on the lip of the gorge, this big tree stump . . . and on it is a huge pile of shit."

I smiled and shook my head no.

"*Human* shit. An immense pile of it. And . . . it had just *rained.* So it was kind of . . . soggy. I saw it and a *chill* went up my spine and I thought, Why has this been done to me? Why must I view this?"

"It was a sign of something," I said.

"You tell me," said Jim.

"No."

"I got to class a little late and there wasn't anybody there. I went to the office of the gal I was assisting and I said, 'What's up?' She glared at me. I said, 'What am I supposed to do?' and she said, this is a quote, this is how it happened, 'You can go soak your head in a bucket of water for all I care.' "

"That was how they let you go."

Jim nodded. "I took it upstairs and they told me I was a good teacher but that I was irresponsible, that my attitude was not good. They said they were sorry. I said, You can't imagine what you're doing to me, the extent of the damage you will cause, my self-esteem, my checkbook, the *furniture* van is—my *wife* just got here, my rental deposit—sorry sorry sorry."

"Did you get any licks in?"

"I went back downstairs and called her a fascist cunt."

"Well, that's something at least."

"Then I got real sick. Dry heaves. Actually shit in my pants. Sobbing in a motel tub. I keep harking back to the shit on the tree stump."

"How could you have avoided it? Any of it?"

"I might have been better prepared."

I was sure there was more to the story, but I let it go. Jim seemed terrifically saddened by the telling, and sadness was very rare with him. *I* was sad all the time, hypersensitive, more and more afraid of strange people and places, tears welling uncontrollably at the slightest kindness. At the door, I had to adopt a hard, evil regard to protect myself, glaring balefully and speaking to no one, while Jim chattered and joked. He had what we called "a winning way with people," even though we both knew he was profoundly a loser. Gary came down the bar to us. We ordered further shots and talked about basketball until the lights came up and the last patrons departed.

Friends of the band or people who worked there lingered for a few minutes while we closed the place up and dealt with the money. A guy I'd seen out of the corner of my eye a couple of times that night came up to us, blinking in the terrible light, and we recognized him as another high-school acquaintance. His name was Wayne Bamer. Wayne was FYI's manager. Coked-up and intensely jolly, he was beside himself with joy at having met us: the world was so small.

It seemed to me that Wayne had hit a zenith in the seventh or eighth grade. He was the kind of tough guy who was able to court persons from all cliques, who could make a hostile gesture in the hallway seem like the nod of acceptance. Once, he tripped me on the way to homeroom. He and some intimates laughed. I'd just won an intramural wrestling tournament and had some currency, some influence among the cliqueless, so I came back at him instead of continuing to class. The bell rang and my heart beat with fear. Wayne said, "I heard you kicked ass, man, way to go," and stopped me cold. He grabbed my dangling arm and shook my hand. I stammered something and looked into his eyes. Was he saying something else to me? I nodded uncertainly at the ring of thugs and then broke into a trot. I'd just gotten a new wristwatch and involuntarily checked the time. My name trailed after me: *Lance.* Whether in derision or amusement or simple recognition, I could not say.

And there he was in front of me again. Babbling. Nothing at all in the eyes.

"FYI. What could it stand for? Fuck You, Irving? I have other bands as well. You know Ass-mar? From *Lord of the Flies?* The fat kid with glasses who gets offed on the cliff? Because he's got *ass-mar* and can't survive in the wilderness? Asthma? I got Sunny & Chair too. They play here all the time. *Funny? Fuck,* man. I got 'em lined up at Laff Riot. They can weight their show every which way, comedy or old folkie, touching ballads, social commentary. Everyone says *specialize* to them. I think the worst thing they could do is make a choice. On the serious side, I got the Saint Paul Saxophone Quartet."

Derf, the manager, came up on the other side of the bar.

Wayne said, "I keep telling this dickhead he should book the quartet, but jazz, I fear, offends his concept of this saloon."

"Honking and tweeting," said Derf. "The place would clear out like *that.*" He snapped his fingers. *"And no more Sunny & Chair. Ever."*

Wayne turned back to us with a big sigh. "You guys want to be free of this man and his establishment? I got work. Honest, clean stuff. I'll pay you ten an hour. Don't look at me like that. You need work? Money is not a problem. I'm rollin— money is the *least* of my fucking worries."

The work consisted of taking crowbars and sledge-hammers to the creepy decayed interior of a house and then installing light and breeziness and modern fixtures. Wayne was never there. He'd come in with sinister and/or dazed professionals of music and related fields, throw open the re-frigerator, and hand beers around, talking fast. Then they would all pile out as they'd piled in. Occasionally, a clear-eyed conservative might be spotted, introduced always as "a true working musician, a serious dude." Even more rarely we would be introduced to financiers. Sometimes these men would be dressed traditionally and well, and sometimes not. Jim and I would look up from the basement, through the bare ceiling beams, at these men clapping across the loose plywood that served as a floor, and Wayne would shout names, and beer would fall to us, the soft aluminum cans indenting in our palms. The men would look over the edge of the plywood and see our round chalky faces staring up at them. Often, they would say nothing, saluting with their cans, and Jim and I would return to the concrete wall we were slugging down, return to the sheetrock and spackling guns, return to the cop-per tubing, torch, solder, and flux, the acetylene flame pure and blue in the musty dusty dark. Wayne paid us in cash every Friday afternoon at three.

We kept up the greeting at the 500 for a couple of reasons

I now see as equally and deeply suspect. Number one was, we did not want to become carpenter monks. For Jim, it was simple: he needed to talk to people. Talking freed him of thought. I was trying to face down a comprehensive fear, a fear of "unsatisfactory social exchanges" (so it was explained to me). I felt limited in my resources, limited to the point where I could not deal with rudeness or even frankness, to the point where I believed I could never explain myself or my position to the other party, to the point where I did not believe the other party had the slightest interest in explanations of position, of right and wrong, of integrity and expediency, to the point where I felt violence imminent, not as the last resort, but as the *only* resort, to the point where I felt violence inhering in every isolated incident, from a request for cash back at the bank to a lane change. I thought, I have to keep coming back to the door. If I stay in the basement now, I'll never come up.

Reason number two was, we were getting caught up in the idea of steady work, of working all day and all night, eating simple meals and sleeping the good sleep of laborers, getting up and working. We also began to save our money. We were getting caught up in the idea of that, too. There was less and less we wanted. We began to compete with each other to see who could go the longest without an expenditure. We stopped drinking. Jim began to speak of leaving his wife, the first sign we might have perceived as "bad," while I spoke of leaving town. These comprised our preoccupations: the abandonment of responsibility and a thing we referred to in shorthand as "the coast of Labrador."

Jim lost a small bet to me (we gambled with each other freely, but only with each other, and did not view the money as "spent") when he purchased a sleeping bag good to 40 below and a foldup cot. He handed me the ten and said, "Buy me a drink, will you? I feel I should celebrate."

"Why?"

"She left me."

"Oh."

"No more hissing through clenched teeth. No more horrifying skull faces. No more weeping all night. No more planning. No more hope for the future."

Sometime later, Jim said, "I read somewhere in my researches that the ultimate test of a man is what he'd do if he knew he could get away with it."

I made a farting sound.

"What would you do?" asked Jim.

"I don't know. What would you do?"

"I don't know."

"Lie?"

"I suppose," said Jim. "I mean, I certainly do *now* . . ."

"Cheat?"

"That would depend on whom I was cheating."

"Say me," I said.

"No." He wagged his head in drunken certitude.

"Rob a bank?"

"Yes." Equal certitude.

"Kill somebody?"

"Again, that depends."

"Of course," I said.

"If I hated this person and they deserved to die? Yes."

"I agree with you. But I think it would be hard to stop. Wouldn't it? Once you got going?"

"Maybe you're right," said Jim.

Gary walked by with drinks on a tray for some friends of his (there were no waitresses and normally only service at the bar), and we plucked them off the tray. We downed them and smiled like idiots, foundering in dreams of impunity. Gary looked on as only the sober can. We produced our savings passbooks and extrapolated figures until last call.

On April Fools' Day, I went over to Wayne's and found Wayne and Jim having coffee in the bathroom we'd tiled the day before. Wayne looked eager and dazed, as if he hadn't slept in forty nights, and gave off a tremendous rotting smell. His clothes were limp and soiled.

"We're going to construct a sound studio *here,*" he said with odd emphasis, as if he meant the bathroom. "State-of-the-art, etc. You know anything about burglar alarms, Lancey? Billion dollars' worth of jazz and shit. Fuck it, why not armed fucking *guards?*"

And he went out and bought two Doberman pups. For starters. To initiate the posture of security.

"Go to the library and read up. Do some consulting. We can do this by ourselves. I'm so sick and tired of relying on other assholes. People will always let you down if they possibly can. Always, always, always. You guys I trust. Plus, I'm devoting all my time to this. Everything else is on hold. Jimmy's already living here, we got a bedroom finished, and this is now my home. I'm bringing my lady in. I want to start a family. Here's the bad news. I can't pay you for this week and you're gonna have to start this bastard on faith. Will you?"

"Hell, yes," said Jim, holding his coffee cup to his cheek.

"Shit-yeah," I said in the Northern manner, making it a single word. "We're having the time of our lives."

Wayne mostly talked, and we never saw "his lady." Though we heard her stomping angrily about or crying at regular intervals. Hysteria was in the air like perfume. Visitors thinned out. In the background was a constant faint bickering.

The weather finally turned. The lakes melted. Wayne was finding money and we got paid off and on. Then one of his cars was stolen. It was an old car, his junk-hauling car, but Wayne was enraged, truly scary about it, acting at times almost as if he thought we'd taken it just to torment him. When he got the call that it had been found, up north in Motley, he was ecstatic. It had been cleaned out (tools mostly and a pair of ice skates) and run into a ditch, but it was damaged only superficially, and the Highway Patrol had towed it to the county seat at Little Falls, where it was being stored. Wayne leapt about his half-finished house, called his lady, almost sobbing with relief into the phone, then called up to Little Falls to arrange the retrieval. He was informed that yes, they had his car, and yes, he could pick it up anytime during business hours after he had paid the hundred-dollar towing and storage fee.

"Wait—hang on a sec. It was stolen. I didn't steal it."

Jim and I watched his emaciated face darken.

"I didn't leave it in the fucking ditch! Find the cocksucker who left it in the fucking ditch! Try getting him to pay the fucking towing and fucking storage!"

Wayne placed calls to his district representative and state senator, and spoke moderately of his disappointment that such a practice existed in the state of Minnesota. Then he called the sheriff in Little Falls and let him have it. Wayne was assured that his insurance company would pay for it, but this meant little to him, as he had no insurance.

Finally, we all went up there and got it. Wayne needed only one of us to drive, but he said he wanted friends near who could help him bang heads off the wall if anybody looked at him cross-eyed.

Nobody did, but it was good to get out of the city. We talked recklessly of get-rich-quick schemes that ran the gamut from wild investments to convenience-store holdups. Wayne inspired this kind of thinking. He was edgy and resourceful and doomed, and it was clear where the money—most of it, if not all—came from. He was an "outlaw," and we were "hard-luck cowboys."

I bought a fishing rod and a tent. Jim was informed by his estranged wife that she was pregnant. It brought on wave after wave of sadness in him, and took the life out of his speech. Wayne came to us in those last days of our association, meekly and without funds. He wanted a favor that would make everything better.

"Person X owes Person Y tons and tons of money. Person

X is fundamentally an asshole. Person X is moving up in the world and thinks that this renders all debts to Person Y void. I promise you, absolutely no violence will be involved. Is that what you're thinking? It's not the kind of deal in which so much is at stake that violence will accrue. I promise this. I'm not in the habit of endangering myself. Life is too short. And you guys are the last guys in the world I would put in jeopardy. But. I want to make a tiny show for Person X. *Just be there with me.* Knock on the door after I've been in there for five minutes and he'll just *see* that business is business. He is not a criminal type and neither am I. We've been scared before and we'll be scared again. *It works.* Fear is one of the things you can count on to work. It's old-fashioned and effective, and so am I. All I need is your support. Come in looking grim—you guys both look pretty grim, I don't need to tell you. It's no surprise to you, is it, that I deal? I don't know. Life is too short to deal."

It wasn't a surprise, but it was disconcerting to hear I looked grim.

Jim and I sat in the junk hauler, feet surrounded by beer bottles and fast-food packaging, cigarette butts and empty oil cans. It was midnight and we were in the suburbs west of the city. The windows of the car were open, but there was nothing to hear beyond the faint drone of traffic on the belt line a half mile off. Brief spells of wind went through the trees (two big cottonwoods, sometimes referred to as "talking trees"), and the leaves rubbed and sighed. I saw a rabbit in a circle of pale purple yard light and pointed it out to Jim, who nodded thoughtfully.

"We can just go," I said. "This is silly."

"Sure," he said. "You want to?"

But we didn't.

The house had been dark when we pulled in the driveway. Wayne had gone to the door and knocked in a certain way. Then, soundlessly, there was a second dark form at the door.

We heard nothing and then Wayne was inside. We waited for a longish time.

"How long did he say to wait?"

"Five minutes is what he said," said Jim.

"How long has it been?"

"I don't know." He tried to read his watch. "Let's say five from now."

We waited another fifteen. No lights came on, we heard nothing, nothing changed.

"Well, *Christ,*" said Jim.

"He didn't say anything about a *sign,* did he?"

"Wait five, knock and enter."

"Jesus fucking Christ," I said.

"Let's just go and knock, then, goddamnit."

"Fucking bloody hell."

And then we were at the door and out of ourselves completely, ready to smile and make gestures of submission. I touched the doorknob and we listened. Jim nudged me and I turned to him. He made an impatient comical face. I must have looked frightened, because his face fell. We stood there, watching ourselves wait and tremble, and then the fear became anger, as it often will. I stepped back and then pounded as hard as I could. Then we moved to either side of the door, ready to snarl and/or bolt into the suburban night. When nothing came of it, we sighed and opened the door.

"Hello!" I said.

"Anybody home?" Jim.

"Hello in there!" Me.

"Hey!" Jim.

"Hey, hey, hey!" Me.

"Hello, goddamnit!" Jim.

"Find a fucking cocksucking light," I whimpered.

We found them in the living room. Wayne and Asshole X sat in opposite stuffed chairs. The conversation of death was still in the air. We walked in somehow and I squeezed a tiny amount of shit into my underwear. Jim was hyperventilating.

There was a small pistol in Asshole X's hand, a slightly larger pistol on the floor near Wayne's limp arm. His mouth was pursed as if he was going to make a judicious point, and his eyes were half open. There was blood. There was blood and two dead assholes, a couple of revolvers and a thick cylinder of rolled bills. Jim made a small choked sound and grabbed the money. I said, "Wait, there may be more," and there was.

I never saw Jim again. I bought another rod and an electric trolling motor. We never got caught, but of course there are worse things than getting caught. There is always the feeling that you have done something you should not have done, and that, further, it happened without warning. You were deaf, dumb, and blind, and did not know even yourself. Knew nothing, had no control, no control of any of it at all. **Q**

KATHERINE ARNOLDI

Crosscut Saw

All this is silent.

Sixty-seven people dressed in black walk single file through a field of snow. The sky is overcast, white. It should be someplace like Kansas, so it can be flat with no horizon. The people curlicue through the field of snow and stop at the side of a lake where a bus overturned a few hours before. They stare at a hole in the ice. A blue diaper bag pops to the surface and someone lifts it and sloshes it onto the ice. Then a watermelon bobs to the surface. Someone stoops, lifts the watermelon, and, cradling it in both hands, leads the sixty-seven people all dressed in black single file through the field of snow and back to the town.

I don't live in Kansas. I live on Avenue C in New York City. The rest of this is noisy.

My ex-lover told stories better than any of yours.

My ex-lover has brown eyes with a blue ring around the edge and he sees two ways, between and through, and has three ways of being, depending on the drug. In 1964, he dyed his hair silver to match his guitar, but just before a gig, it all fell out, and that was his story.

My friend Anna senses things through her feet. Once, when we were standing in front of the Second Avenue Deli, she told me that her lover had stood in that exact spot an hour before kissing a new lover, and she was right, because I was across the street and saw it all.

"So what?" I said. "That's a pointless waste of good feet. Why can't you tell fortunes or something useful?" Two days later, when we were bringing back shrimp fried rice from Hop Fat's, she stopped in the middle of Avenue C, backed up a few steps, and told my future up until March 2, 1999, and everything has come true so far.

My ex-lover was strong and good. Once he jumped off a cliff and fell chest-first through the air and then glided into a river without a ripple.

I have just told a lie. My ex-lover was fifty, has emphysema, and brown, gutted teeth. He is weak and frail. He passed out every night.

"Do your teeth hurt?" I asked him once when he brought them up.

"Hell, no," he said. "If one hurts, I get it taken out."

The people in the field were Mennonite, which explains their dress. I myself am Mennonite and this year I planned to go to the Passover feet-washing ceremony, but instead stayed home to be by the phone.

"He won't call," Anna says.

"Is that from your feet or your head?" I say.

"My feet."

"Damn," I say.

He sang, "I'm a crosscut saw. Honey, drag me cross your log. I'll cut your wood so easy, can't help but say hot dog," but as I already mentioned, he passed out every night.

The Mennonite feet-washing ceremony goes like this: The women get up from the church pews and go to the basement. We sit in rows of folding chairs. The first woman in a row squats on her knees and washes the next woman's feet. She uses Ivory soap and dries the feet with a towel. Then both women stand, embrace, and kiss each other. Nobody talks until all the feet are washed.

My ex-lover sang about evil in your home, staying high all the time, do-wang-wang doodling all night, and going back to get his old gal Sue. His baby's long. His baby's tall. When she lays down in the kitchen, her feets stick way out in the hall.

I'm long and tall.

My great-grandmother was a doctor in Ohio, and she traveled alone to Illinois to live with the Indians and improve her art. There she married an Indian man and brought him back to her Mennonite community. She was at someone's bedside being a doctor when she looked up and said, "My husband just died, I have to go home."

"I want a VCR," my ex-lover said one morning. Within an hour, he named thirteen things he wanted. A turntable. A van. A new hat. His five-month-old child, who was taken away from the mother and put in foster care because it was born with a cocaine dependency. A new suit. A set of wineglasses. A new kitchen table. "This one rocks," he said.

Every Thursday we would go to the Social Services Center, and the foster parent would bring the child to our cubicle for an hour. "He cries all night. Nothing but fussing with this one here," the foster parent says.

It's February, cold. My ex-lover and I stand on Avenue A. A bowlegged person comes at us holding up what looks like an old dryer hose attached to a smashed electrical apparatus. "I came by it on a fluke," he says to us. "I came by it on a fluke," he says to the heavens. "I came by it on a fluke," he says over and over down Third Street.

"I came by everything the same way," my ex-lover says, and kisses me.

Then the mother of the child got out of jail. "You two get married, get the child," I said, and packed everything in a Glad trash bag. My robe. My quilt. The box of Lipton tea I'd bought. "You owe me forty-three backrubs," I said.

"Could we make that forty-four?" he said.

Anna and I are thirty-seven. I draw hearts with fake valves and knees with plastic parts for medical publications. Anna makes hats and word-processes. For fifteen years we have been like this. As though we are lying on moss-covered rocks in a creek shaded by willow and sycamore trees. As though we have our feet together and our heads cushioned on opposite banks. As though we've watched our lovers pass over our bodies like water and float downstream, far under the horizon. **Q**

No, Cup

Get the family out forever, out from around the table.

Now, at breakfast, the most important objects on the table are the way-out-of-whack coffee cups for the parents, twice normal size, and their double-sized saucers, all shiny black.

The cups are almost as tall as the normal-sized white pitcher of milk that was there for the children, when the children were there.

The white paper napkin, not nearly as important as the cups are, partially hidden under the biscuits in the basket, and getting soiled by biscuit grease, is sticking up. The points at the corners of the napkin are what stick up the highest, but the points do not reach as high as the white milk pitcher reaches with its lips—*pardon,* lip. Even so, allow for the possibility that both the lip of the pitcher and the napkin points express human aspiration, conceptually.

Already, there is too much to think about on the table. What is the most important thing? One of the cups should be enough to think about.

Cup.

The shine on the cup.

Light.

No, *cup.*

The most important thing in any circumstance is what people want to believe is all wrong, you asshole.

Defecation. **Q**

Characterize

The hostess created them in their image.

The cookies are turkeys inscribed with edible names on the butter plates.

There are two cooked, twelve-pound turkeys, no longer in those images, on platters for the entree, waiting.

The guests are waiting for the entree, discussing the weather, because winter has not arrived, and one month previous to this time, it should have. (This time, in this place, the winter never does arrive.)

The comments of a husband and a wife about how they feel about the weather prove dramatically to any omniscient thinker that they are dramatically unsuitable, maritally, for one another.

Their infant, who can understand their language better than his own, is listening.

A catastrophic earthquake occurs on another continent in a geographical zone that has never harbored a vicious winter. This is in the country Turkey. There they have certainly had a number of earthquakes in the regions where the winter is mild and only rainy and in those other regions as well.

That's how the cookie crumbles.

No, seriously, my darling, "thou art my bone and my flesh." **Q**

Cannibal, the Natural History

Everything was so bad because of what happened in the spring, but I eat it.

I asked Chuck, "What happened in the spring?"

Something very very bad. I couldn't get to what without Chuck's help. The reason to remember was to keep talking to Chuck for X amount of time.

Chuck said, then I nearly said, the *drought.* He said it first.

"Is there good news?" I asked Chuck.

I did not address Chuck as Chuck, who was unaware I knew his name or his secret.

Chuck answered me spitefully. "They are ripening them artificially."

Spiteful Chuck. I knew. The secret about Chuck was that everything was nice about Chuck except that he did not know how—*anything* about being nice. Something else about eating—the train of my thought—in X amount of time, nowhere near Chuck, I got to it—it was mothers who would not knowingly eat a coward before their babies were born. Among these people, the diet restrictions were severe. Strict for a purpose.

I'm a mom like that. Not to brag, today at lunch, Maggie did not smell it on me, what I have been cooking. She guessed wrong. *Chuuuuuuck!*

I know one thing about Maggie. She is a very, very mixed-up person. **Q**

Right Out of a Machine

I can feel her up there. I can feel her motion. She's walking back and forth past my window. And then she's just standing, looking down, trying to see through my curtains. To see me lying in my bed. And then she moves again. There're bars on the window, there's no way she can get in. But the thought of her. I lie here, not moving an inch, not making a sound. I'm trying so hard to hear her. But I can't. I can only feel her. Every once in a while, I can hear my heart, or I can hear one of the mice gnawing in the walls. The mice she brought with her.

She's out in the alley between the two houses, waiting for her fifty dollars.

I came home one day and she was on my porch, just sitting there. She looked basic, without a home, crazy. I smiled at her and nodded as I came up the stairs. "Hi," I said. It's all I wanted to do, say hi, walk in, never see her again.

Why *my* porch?

"I'm looking for my father," she said, wiggling her hands over the paper bag she was holding. "He lives here," she said.

She was older than me. She was just older.

"There are no fathers here," I said, and shut the door on her. She had gotten up and was ready to walk in. There weren't any fathers. There was a college couple on the first floor and waitresses on the second. Then me in the basement.

That night I wondered if she was sleeping on the porch, but mostly I made dinner and went to sleep. I thought about getting her a blanket, but mostly I was sleeping. The next morning, I didn't see her. She wasn't on the porch. I drove to work, worked, and on the way home, I drove into town to go to the bank machine. There she was outside the bank machine. She didn't say anything or look at me. I put my card in the slot and the door buzzed and I got to go inside, and she didn't try to come in. Her face was dirty and I was taller.

When I came out, she said, "Do you have some dollars you can give me?" She held out her bag to me. I couldn't see anything in it. It just looked black inside it.

She was smart to stand in front of the bank machine like that.

I almost got run over crossing the street.

That night, again, I made dinner, tuna and crackers. I read a comic book I found in the garbage at work. I went to bed. I woke up, but it was still night and I heard voices upstairs. Up on the porch. I can hear stuff on the porch from my room. I heard her voice and one of the waitresses telling her, You can't stay here, you can't stay here. I heard Mandy or Minda say she would call the police.

I felt better.

The next morning, when I went to my car, she came out at me from between the two houses. It was just a little misty and she had sparkles of rain in her hair. I walked to my car fast.

That night, I lay in the dark listening for her. I couldn't hear anything, and then I did. I heard a noise like a mouse in the wall, chewing. Chewing his way through the wall, a mouse bite at a time.

I went to the wall and the noise stopped.

That's how she'll do it, I thought. She'll have the mice gnaw their way in and she'll crawl through. I'll come home to find her sitting on my kitchen floor, eating tuna and crackers, reading my comic book, cackling. There will be mice all over, running around in tuna cans.

I didn't sleep that night, but I found Mouse-Kill in the linen closet. I put it under the sink and behind my record player.

The next day, I saw a dollar in the road. I parked on top of it and felt great. I lay down on the sidewalk and reached under my car. It was a fifty—dry, straight, and crisp. Right out of a machine.

She can't find her father.

I put the money in my pocket.

I'm afraid I'll be too tired to work tomorrow. It's three already. I fall asleep and then I wake up. I can hear my heart beating. I can hear the mouse chewing. But it's slower every time I wake up. It must've reached the poison. It'll never make it to my side of the wall. I haven't spent the money. I doze off, but I have this dream. Two arms come crashing through the window above my bed. Glass sparkles in my eyes. **Q**

A History of My Life

Down in the whippersnaps, knee-high, where the land is wet and almost everyone is in some kind of trouble, that was where I came from, unbeknownst even to myself. Down there may be where I will end up, in trouble, underneath the gray sky and in the wet rain.

It was mid-day and not quite spring. A fog surrounded everyone and their brains. Not a voice was heard, but there were the permanent rustlings of nerves. Nowhere I have been are there people and silence at the same time. People, plants, and animals make sounds, unrehearsed.

I was a child from a mill town that was losing business, and Jack Kennedy was our congressman. The war was over and the adults were having children. Uranium was a new concept, and room was made for it.

I lay in a stroller on our porch in the dead white winter, and had fat red cheeks. There were baskets of us all up and down the blocks. We were the hope of America, and then came the Russians.

The sixties: you remember the assassinations. I remember coming the first time into my own hand, and being told to think of college. But no one on our block knew college. All we knew were jobs and Johnny Unitas. A girl, Kim, got pregnant and there was a lot of hushed-up talk. Thank God for the Beatles and for that yellow shirt and tie that made me proud to be at Mass. I was going to be somebody. I had a sneaking feeling.

For almost everyone I know well, it was about then that life began, the insertion of a few lyrics between the braces. A completely new-seeming credo broke like a Coke bottle, even despite the assassinations. I left home and took a bus and went to Alaska, fighting forest fires. I was skinny and lost twenty more pounds just familiarizing myself with the country. I came back East and tried Chinese food for the first time, meanwhile telling my first successful lies. They left imprints, so I lived that way for a long time, eluding something, blaming it on the Congress and the cuisine.

My father died in 1980, and I had a job with free-floating coffee breaks. I was already looking back. Without a wife, I seemed to stand guilty. Road races gave me a certain standing. But as the eighties heated up, I thought of the girl, Kim, who had got pregnant. What had happened to Kim? And what about the kid? Oh, Jesus.

I would come to some conclusion if I could. I turn four–zero soon, and live in no neighborhood. It is something, being always on the high tide of history and trying to whistle like all the other fish. We would plot if we knew how, but instead we let the water just get sucked through us. I am astounded every day by all the newborns. **Q**

Fishing Trips

I

Jim and Sam have planned the trip for months. The equipment shows this—the topographical maps mailed away for, the complicated first-aid kit, the nesting camper's cookware. All the equipment has been secured, wrapped in plastic, and taped or lashed in the twenty-one-foot aluminum canoe. The canoe has been painted bright red. Jim says this is to ensure visibility if the canoeists are lost. Sam holds the opinion that the bright color makes the canoe look as if it were made of fiberglass instead of aluminum. They didn't ask the man at the outfitter's where they rented the canoe two days ago. The issue becomes irrelevant now, when they are in the middle of a deep lake and the canoe strikes a submerged rock or log. The fishermen paddle quickly when this happens and the bottom of the canoe tears open.

The fishermen are saved by their fisherman's vests, the multipocketed, khaki-colored flotation devices they bought at K mart for this trip. They bob momentarily in the water, gasping and coughing, still shocked at how the canoe has sunk out from under them.

Jim calls, Are you okay?

Sam nods.

Both turn their heads and look along the shoreline.

Where should we head for? Jim says.

Sam tries to shrug, but he just bobs.

The fishermen swim for shore. Their vests keep them afloat, but the devices also seem awkward. The pine trees look distant, and it's hard for the fishermen to tell how much progress they're making.

Finally, the fishermen reach shore. There is a sandy area perhaps ten feet wide, and behind it weeds and grasses, and behind them the forest. Jim and Sam sit on the beach, panting.

By Sam's watch it is 10:49 A.M. The air is warm and Jim esti-
mates the temperature to be in the low seventies. Sam unzips
his vest and pulls it off. He rolls it up, lies back, and uses it for
a pillow. Jim imitates Sam. The fishermen lie there, looking at
the sky. Jim takes a soaked and wrinkled cigarette package
from his shirt pocket. He tears open the top and removes a
broken cigarette.

Sam says, Is that the last one?

Jim tears off part of the cigarette and hands it to Sam. He
lights each of their cigarettes with a lighter. The tobacco sput-
ters and the paper bleeds brown, but the wet cigarettes stay lit.

When they've finished, Sam says, How far in are we?

Hard to say, Jim says.

I think it'll be awhile before they look for us, Sam says. I
mean weeks, Sam says. He stands up, then squats down on his
heels. He empties his pockets. Sam has a red bandana, a small
Swiss army knife, some keys, and a ballpoint pen. Jim has the
same things, except instead of the ballpoint pen he has the
cigarette package and lighter, and he finds a small plastic box
of hooks in the Velcro-sealed pocket of his fishing vest.

We'll make it. Sam looks around. He picks up the bandana
and frays one edge of it with his knife. He tears it into thin
strips. We'll knot these together for line.

They'll see the knots.

They won't know they're knots. Think of the Indians.
They didn't have monofilament.

Okay, Jim says. I'll get poles. He walks into the forest. He
is back in minutes with some gnarled sticks. Sam shakes his
head. The best I could do, Jim says. The fishermen bait their
hooks with aluminum foil from the cigarette package. After
hours, the fishermen have two small fish. The fishermen take
the fish with them when they go for firewood.

The camp seems permanent. The utensils, a few tin
cans and two rough wooden trenchers, are near the fire ring.

The lean-to looks solid. Two fishing poles are rigged in forked sticks, and Jim is trying to make a trotline of braided tree bark while Sam experiments with small deadfall traps. The fishermen have been keeping a calendar, but the fishermen didn't start until they realized they didn't know how long they had been there. The fishermen have not seen any other people, but they are confident that people canoe through this area all the time. The food is monotonous: fish, boiled acorns, dandelions, wild strawberries. The fishermen try to watch what the birds eat. The fishermen believe that any plant a bird can eat will not be poisonous to humans. The water in the lake is good.

The fishermen have seen deer and a moose in the forest, and have found bear tracks near their camp. The bear tracks concern the fishermen. Jim wants to move up from the beach into the forest. Sam agrees that this might be wise, but he feels the fishermen should be near the fish and water of the lake. He suggests that the fires and human scent will keep the bears away. Jim says the fishermen should move on, perhaps circle the lake in hopes of finding some other people.

That, Sam says, is going against what they say. They say you should stay put and wait for help. He goes on to point out that the bear, or bears, have not come into the camp.

Jim goes into the forest and comes back with a birch sapling. He sharpens one end of the trunk and hardens the point in the fire. Sam watches him. Later, he makes a spear like Jim's.

The fishermen work together, using the wooden hoe and shovel they've fashioned to make a deer trap. The fishermen dig a trench and plant stakes with fire-hardened points in it.

Early the next morning, a deer falls into their trap. The deer is still alive. One of its forelegs is stuck through with a spike and there are two spikes in its abdomen. Its tongue hangs out and it shakes its head from side to side. Kill it, Sam says. Jim swings his spear at the animal. The blow hits the deer on the flank and lifts the deer off the spikes. The deer jerks its legs. It tries to stand. Sam swings his spear at the deer's head.

Jim stabs the deer in the side and Sam smashes it on the neck. The fishermen keep doing this until the deer lies on its side, its wounded leg nearly severed, its coat covered with blood and dust. The fishermen stand there looking at the deer.

They bleed and skin the deer and decide to cook it whole in hopes that the meat will keep longer cooked. The fishermen spit the deer on a green branch over a fire pit. Jim sets the heart and liver on hot rocks. He turns the organs after a few minutes. Sam tears the liver into two pieces and gives one to Jim. Jim tears the heart and hands a piece to Sam.

The carcass chars on the outside. Sam rips off a strip of meat. The inside is still raw. The fishermen break off pieces of the burnt layer and eat, making their way inward.

II

After the first or second winter, Jim spots the tracks. It is morning, a little after dawn, and Jim is out to check some snares and the trotline. Sam is in camp, rubbing deer brains on a stretched hide. There are two sets of tracks. Both were made by the cleated synthetic soles of hiking boots.

Jim listens. He can't hear anything. He follows the tracks for a few yards, then stops again. Again he hears nothing. He follows the tracks like this for an hour or more, then backtracks to camp.

Sam and Jim follow the tracks until they hear voices. The fishermen dive into the brush. The fishermen wait for a while and then crawl until they reach the top of a small rise. The fishermen look down into the clearing where the man and woman have set up camp. The fishermen see an orange nylon tent and a backpacker's stove that burns bottled gas. They see a red fiberglass canoe next to the tent and a box of groceries hanging from a tree.

Sam motions toward the trail. He and Jim creep back slowly, then run to their own camp.

The fishermen come back that night. They wait to be sure

no one is moving. The fishermen make their way down the rise, pick up the canoe, and run up the trail. No one comes after them.

III

By the end of the summer, the fishermen have two canoes, fishing rods, knives, and axes. They don't bother with food or clothing, although once Sam took a salt shaker.

Two fishermen are camped a few miles away. Sam and Jim have scouted the camp. The new fishermen leave early each morning and return at midday with their catch. It seems likely that the new fishermen have liquor, and it is always possible they will have guns.

Sam and Jim wait for a few hours after the sun has risen and go to the new fishermen's camp. They follow the trail and walk straight into the center of the camp. Jim cuts the box of groceries down from a tree and searches through it. Sam splits the side of the green tent with a fillet knife. He jumps back as the man inside jumps up. The tent is caught around the new fisherman's legs. He frees himself and runs past Sam to the woodpile. Sam runs after him. The new fisherman grabs a piece of birch from the pile and swings it at Sam. Sam stabs the fisherman in the stomach. Jim is behind the fisherman. Jim has a piece of wood. The fisherman stumbles forward and swings the stick again. It hits Sam in the face. Jim beats the man's head while Sam stabs.

IV

The chase goes on for days. Jim and Sam see a few of the men. The men wear camouflage clothing and carry guns. They have dogs. Jim and Sam burn what will burn in camp and throw the rest in the lake. The fishermen paddle the canoes out to the middle of the lake, sink one, and take the other to the opposite shore. They sink it in a few feet of water and go inland. The fishermen climb trees and keep watch.

At first, they are safe on the opposite shore. But then they hear dogs barking. Sam and Jim run. The fishermen run for hours, dodging through the woods. They look for water—streams, ponds, puddles—anything to throw off the scent. The dogs are behind the fishermen. After a while, they stop hearing the dogs. At night, the fishermen walk as quickly as they can down the open trails. Sometimes the fishermen crawl into thickets to sleep.

One morning, the fishermen see a lake, blue in the sun, below them as they stand on a wooded bluff. The fishermen are looking for a path to the water when the helicopter comes over them. The fishermen run along the bluff, see a steep path, scramble down. They hear dogs. At the base of the bluff there is a strip of woods and the narrow rocky beach. Sam and Jim dodge through the trees, looking back, looking up, looking for the helicopter. The fishermen cannot see or hear it. They hear only the hunters. The fishermen scramble over the rocks. They see the hunters. The hunters fire and keep firing. Jim grabs his abdomen and falls, bleeding. His body tumbles as it is hit. Sam jumps into the water and swims. **Q**

The Story

Frank had a dynamite story. Monica was telling him, "Frank, tell Al the story. Al, you sticking with rye? Frank honey, let me get you another." She kind of waves at us with her hand and all those pink bracelets jangle. Pink bracelets, pink nails, pink lipstick, and shiny pink pants that are stuffed just right.

Monica is something.

Frank and Monica were drinking martinis. Frank used to be a rye drinker. We'd sit out on his deck drinking ryes past sundown, talking love and oil prices—always bad news—two subjects we could go on and on about without ever having much to do with either. Or we'd end up just drinking and not saying much of anything and feeling fine about that, too. But May around here in Calgary, the wind can kick up something awful, so this time we were all inside.

Frank met Monica on a singles cruise last February. She wasn't quite single at the time, just separated from her second husband. Frank was taking my advice. His scrap-metal business had just about stopped dead for the winter, though he had plenty of dough stashed away from the past couple of boom years. So I told him to take the cruise. That was where Patti and I met, on a cruise. Frank was wearing a Calgary Olympics pin through the heart of the alligator on his shirt and Monica asked him if he'd been there, so Frank told her he lived there, and suddenly, look who couldn't look a lady in the eye his whole life and is now strolling moonlit decks with a blond, bikinied bombshell. She was running away from Red Deer, Monica told Frank, from Barney, her first husband's ex–best friend, but who knows, she told Frank, they're probably buddy-buddy again, swapping whore-Monica jokes together at some pissant minor-league hockey game. As for Frank, he was just running away from being Frank, Monica had been telling me, and just maybe he got away clean, she says. Then she takes our drink orders and says for us to sit tight.

"Some girl, eh?" says Frank. "Ever think I'd marry a girl like Monica?"

"Hell, Frank," I tell him. "Who'da ever thought anybody'd ever marry you?"

"That's right," says Frank. "But it's amazing the change in me. Hey, you notice I dropped about fifteen pounds?"

Frank was in deep. Frank was in over his head. Frank didn't know sharks in the water when they bit him, and Monica bit. Me, I been swimming with them a long time. It's wives like Monica got me where I am today. It's the business. You go door-to-door selling home improvements and you get to know these women. You learn to look around and find the little things they do to fix up the house. Then you tell them how great it is, what an artistic streak they have, how their husbands must've loved what they did to the place. And of course, that's the key. You learn to pick the things that nobody, least of all a husband, would notice. A little conversation, a little suggestion here and there, a little fake blush when you let them catch you looking them over, and suddenly you're into their dreams and they got their names on a contract. Then comes the hard part—when you got to sit down man-to-man and explain to the hubby what all this does for him. It's best to act a little swish with them. You sell dreams coming true to the women, interior decorating to the men. And sometimes, over coffee in the kitchen, the wife would reach over and I'd feel a squeeze on my knee and the invitation. It's dreams, TV dreams.

So I say, "Well, Frank. This is it, eh? It doesn't bother you, those other husbands?"

"Hell, Al," says Frank, "I think it's better this way, you know? She's had those other guys to compare me to and, hey, she still wants me."

Monica comes back in with the drinks and the martini pitcher on a tray. "My ears are bur-ning," she sings. She looks over at Frank and cocks her head. Then over at me and clucks her tongue. "What's he been saying about me?"

Frank looks up like an eager pet, big round-eyed stupid puppy smile. "Just telling Al how perfect you are," Frank says.

Monica walks over and bends from the waist, offering me my drink like a cocktail waitress. "Al's a little worried about me, isn't he?" she says, looking at me good and proper.

"Al's a good friend, honey," Frank says.

"That's what I meant, Frank." Then she looks away from me. "You worried, baby?"

"Do I look worried?" says Frank, looking worried.

Monica gets rid of the tray and swivels into the Barcalounger, pops it back and gets her legs crossed on the footpads. Pink toenails, too. "Al, look at that man," she says. "Frank, you've got nothing to worry about, honey," she says.

Newlyweds.

I used to do that stuff for Patti. We were married twenty-seven months.

"So come on, Frank," Monica says. "Tell Al the story."

Frank says, "Al doesn't want to hear that story."

"Sure, I do," I say.

Monica pops the Barcalounger upright and hunches forward, staring at Frank like he's on TV.

"Okay, okay," says Frank. "See, Al, I was downtown last Friday, and I'm stopped at a light and I see a guy walking and wearing long johns and one of those old leather pilot hats with goggles and this big towel he's got tied around his neck for a cape."

"And army boots. Don't forget the army boots," says Monica.

"Right," says Frank, "I almost forgot. And army boots. So, anyway, he's going along real slow with these real long steps and I can see he must be measuring something off. So finally he stops and turns around and he stands there like he's praying for something and then he starts to run. Then he really starts flapping his arms, and then I see him like stick his arms way out and jump. My God, he's laying flat out in the air and I swear he must have been four, five feet off the ground and that's the way he hits—flat out, right on his face, wham. Oh man, what a sight. It's like the guy never even considers that maybe he wouldn't fly."

Monica says to me, "Don't you think that's the craziest thing you ever heard?"

I see Frank just sitting there shaking his head.

So I says, "So what happened next?"

Monica says, "Listen, I'm crazy, too. Like I once bought a new pair of shoes at an Eaton's sale and I wear them twice to go dancing. Second time out, both heels break. Both! So I take them back and the customer service says to me I abused them and won't give me my money back. Fucking abused them! Going dancing? So finally, they got to call the store manager over, because now I'm stretched out over across the service desk pretending to be asleep so's no other customer can get any service until they finish up taking care of me. And, honey," Monica says, "I got my money back, and that's the way I am, you know?"

We sit there for a while, just drinking. Then I reach over to put my glass down on the coffee table, which is over on the other side of the Barcalounger, and Monica says, "Frank honey, your buddy's putting the squeeze on my knee-ee."

And Frank says, "There's nobody else in the world I'd trust to squeeze your knee."

"You trust this old dog?" Monica says, and she winks. "He's a fucking door-to-door salesman."

"Not Al," Frank says.

Monica throws back her head, shaking her blond hair and sort of laughing like that was the funniest thing she ever heard.

But I see Frank look out the window, where the sun is streaming in over the deck. He says, "Just for one second I think I thought the guy might really do it."

We sit there for a while, not saying much, watching the sun

go down, until I lie and say, "I got dinner cooking over at my place and if I don't hurry it'll burn."

I get my jacket. I go out the back way to cut down the alley to my place. I'm in a big hurry to get home. I don't know why. I even start running and taking these big high dumb steps.

Goofy. **Q**

The Son

She walked by it every time she had to come into the room. But she did not touch it. She did not look at it. Whenever she had to move it so that she could clean under it and dust behind it, she would move it, but she would not look at it. She would not lift it, either. She would not touch it with her hands. She would shove it to the side with her legs, or she would lean against it to slide it from the place where it stood. While she was shoving it from the place where it stood, she would not look at it.

On those days when she had to move it, she would look at the rug, at the way the rug was worn in front of it. She would clean the rug in the place where it had stood, the place where the rug was not worn, but then she would shove it back where she could see the worn patch of rug in front of it again—she would shove it back to the place where it always stood. Yes, she had to touch it to move it—but she would touch it with her body, not with her hands, and nothing could ever make her look at it.

At times, when someone came to see her—there were not many who came to see her—she would have to bring the friend into the room where it stood. But even then she would not look at it. The first time that a friend came to see her, came to be with her afterward, she saw the friend walk over to it, make as if to sit down in it, and she quickly said, "Here, here—come here and sit by me, sit by my side." She made herself small in the corner of the sofa where she sat, leaving all the room in the world for the friend. Then she twisted her body in the corner of the sofa in order to see the face of the friend—making certain that she never looked past the friend's face and risked seeing it.

But it was different when he came home. She would see

him walk right into the room where it stood. When he came home for a day or two, she saw him walk right over to it and sit.

"Here, here—come here and sit by me," she would say to him. "On the sofa, close to me," she would say. "No," she said, "I have a better idea. Sit by the window. Sit where I can see you better."

"I can sit right here," she would hear him say. She would see him lean back in it, in that way of his, his shoes digging into the rug in front of it in that way of his.

This is how they sat—she looking at the table in front of her, at the bookshelves, at the window, at everything, but never at him or at where he sat. **Q**

Travelers

We have got all the maps. Pop looks better now. My brother and I share a room.

We have supper with Pop in the kitchen. There is a pickup truck dealer downtown. Out West, they say, you should carry water. We are finished with school for good.

Pop looked okay at suppertime. They let us drive it before we said yes. The doctor asked us if we were twins. We mark the maps so we know how to go.

We have never been out West before. I heard something downstairs in the night. They threw in a wax job at no extra charge. Our house is on a fifty-foot lot.

At supper, Pop said, "I'd like to go with you."

I can see the people next door. Our pickup truck is a custom deluxe. We have pictures of snowcapped peaks.

We go to the Western double features. Our rubber is good all around. In the Southwest the maps have these foreign names. I love Pop very much.

The garbage goes out by the curb in the morning. I got downstairs as fast as I could. There is summer grazing up high, they say. We got a six-month warranty.

I could see the whites of Pop's eyes that night. They repainted our truck at the lot. The doctor says that it could have been worse. We park the truck out in front of the house.

They gave us a tarp that fits over the load. The forest shows green on the maps. We found ads about ranchland in different states. Pop says we are peas in a pod.

Pop kicked in the extra money for us. There were fields once behind the house. I cannot think of Pop alone. The toolbox fits under the seat.

I could see Pop was breathing through his mouth. Out West you can drive any speed. They say that what saved him is we got there so fast. We take turns in the kitchen at night.

The doctor says it could happen again. We have a four-gear stick shift on the floor. Montana, they say, is the best state of all. We are brothers to the bone.

The things for out West are up in the attic. We change the oil every three thousand miles. You can homestead in certain Western states. I think Pop is gaining weight.

My brother and I have been talking. The house needs painting soon. Next door they say not to park on the street. It is almost spring again.

My brother and I are blood brothers in this. The maps are upstairs in our room. **Q**

Old L.A.

It could only happen in this town, or maybe in Bagh-dad or Bangkok. I met an old woman who lived in a shoe. She really did; this is no mere metaphor or fairy tale. I met her on the beach in Venice and she took me home with her, and she lived in a house that had once been a restaurant in the shape of a shoe, then it had gone broke, and now the windows had fallen in and the whole place was dusty and decrepit and smelled like rotten wood, and she lived there with her memo-ries and four cats, one of them so old its spine was paralyzed and it towed its hind legs after it around the house.

The shoe was on La Cienega, but not on the fashionable part of it where all the classy restaurants are, instead far down to the south the other side of Jefferson, where it's pretty tacky now, although as a neighborhood it once had its day. Don't bother trying to find the place; they tore it down long ago and built a video store on the lot.

I was out of a job and couldn't afford the first and last month on an apartment, so I was glad to stay with her for a couple of days. I slept here and there and in other places in the house. There were plenty of places to sleep—niches, al-coves, closets, cupboards. The wind came in through the bro-ken windows and the cracks in the shingles, but that was good, because it drove away the rancid smell that clung to the inside of the place. It smelled exactly like the inside of an old shoe. She slept in the toe, the former kitchen of the restaurant. She had it fixed up quite nice in there: a real bed, a greasy patch-work quilt, an orange pillow with black buttons, and a lamp that looked as though somebody had won it by throwing base-balls at a carnival. I had plenty of chances to observe her room, because the toe of the shoe was where the only toilet in the house was; I had to go into her room and then open a tiny narrow door to get into it. When I left, there was no doubt what I had been doing in there. The toilet made a noise that began with a gentle trickling, like a brook in the springtime, then a gigantic cough, followed by a loud chatter and plashing, louder and softer, up and down, on several musical notes, that echoed through all the rooms of the house until it died away to a murmur. It's funny as I think of it now that, in all the time I stayed in the house, I never heard this sound except when I used the toilet. What she did I don't know. Maybe she just knew some way to work the thing silently.

I stayed there more like a couple of weeks than a couple of days. For sleeping, I finally settled on a shelf that was actually a cupboard with the doors removed. I found some newspapers to put under me and a blanket to go over me; it was really not so bad. After I had gone to bed one night, she appeared in an ancient nightgown that Greta Garbo might have worn in a silent film, and turned the light on. The old woman had the same boyish and sexless frame as the Swedish star, although hers was wrinkled as though a fishnet had fallen over it. Gray hair, white face, black mouth and eyes. Perhaps she herself, I thought, was left over from a silent movie, waiting for someone to colorize her, or if not, to die with nothing but a slight scratching sound, or the indifferent tinkling of a piano. As a matter of fact, she seemed to be in perfect health. Better than mine; I suffered from bronchitis that winter and had a constant cough.

She seemed to live on oatmeal mush, which she made once a week and warmed up every morning. Once, watching her at her breakfast, I was eating a candy bar and I took a raisin out of it and put it on her mush. She ate the raisin, grinned, and said, "Iron. It enriches the blood." She never offered me any of the oatmeal. Instead, in the evening after it grew dark, she fed me chicken broth, producing an old horsewhip and playfully threatening to whip me with it if I didn't do exactly as she said. Then she sent me to bed with a smile that showed the gaps in her broken teeth.

Once I got up to go to the bathroom in the middle of the night, barefoot (I slept in my clothes) and feeling the cats brushing around my shins. As I groped in the dark for the narrow door, she heard me and turned on the kewpie-doll lamp. She said, laughing, "What are you doing in an old woman's room?" Still laughing, she got out of bed and began menacing me with the horsewhip. She made it curl around my toes, playfully, but it hurt. "See how you like that," she said. I did my business and slunk back to my shelf while she watched me in her Greta Garbo gown that showed the tops of her wrinkled dugs. I waited until the hydraulic aria of the toilet had ended, then I went to sleep.

I went out every day, not to look for a job, but to get away from her for a little bit. Sometimes I panhandled a couple of quarters and bought a can of beer in a minimart. She could always detect it on my breath, and said, "Watch out. The first step to doom. Take it from one who knows." But still laughing. She was a gay old thing. I don't know what kept her so merry, except that she had captured me and could make me do whatever she wanted.

After I got to know her a little better, I learned the trick of talking to her, and we had some interesting conversations, cautious on my side, playful on hers. She told me that she had come from Passaic, New Jersey, and was once (just as I thought) an actress. "But they threw me out when sound came in," she said (just as I thought), "because of my voice." "What was wrong with your voice?" "It was like you hear it now."

In time I became playful myself, and asked her why she didn't have so many children that she didn't know what to do. She said, "I hoped that you would make my life fertile." Then she reached for the horsewhip and made me do her will.

I left, but it didn't really bother her. Back to the beach for another one. **Q**

Drives

A family is in a car. The father is driving the car. The father turns the steering wheel, manages the road. The mother tunes the radio. The mother hums. The mother opens a window. The mother's hair is moved by the wind, as is the dress she is wearing. A scrap of paper is moved by the wind, blows around in car, goes out window, goes along road behind car, goes to side of road, goes in ditch.

Mother points to a building off road, behind trees, says, "There it is."

Father looks at son in mirror, smiles.

Mother looks at father, smiles, says, "Edward, do you want your father to stop the car?"

The building is made of stone, with columns, plants along walls, bars across windows, locks on doors. Rooms with beds, rooms with tables, rooms with toys, rooms with machines.

The boy says, "Yes."

Father puts foot on brake, steers car to side of road, stops car, says, "Get out."

Boy puts hand on door handle, pulls handle, pushes door out. Boy puts feet on side of road, steps away from car, closes door.

Mother looks at boy, says, "Edward, they will not take you in."

The boy bends down, picks up rocks from off ground, goes to ditch, crouches down in ditch, drops rocks in front of him.

Mother rolls up window.

Father puts foot on gas pedal, pushes, drives.

Boy, in ditch, picks up rock, keeps rock in hand. **Q**

War Story

Better shoot himself in the foot than go the next hundred miles without rations. The third day of forced march he'd had it. The land was wasted. The joyous army he served took no prisoners; the population was dead men, raped women, and a plague of orphans prowling through the heaps of hides and feathers blood-clotted around the char pits where the potlatch of conquest had gorged itself on every living edible, leaving fuck-all for the rear guard. And winter coming on. Death's metal taste glazed his tongue; after two years of slaying and surviving, he no longer craved the final celebration. The songs they crowed had lost their music. Snow was in the sky; inevitable, streaming, coating the horse he'd seen hung from a door beam, devoured but still the site of battle—boys and girls with sticks fought ravens for the right to suck the bones. In the beginning, he'd been amazed how old the eager thrills and horrors of apocalypse felt, how fast they left him dull, indifferent, their functionary. He'd gone mad, but only later, lately, noticed it, how he'd passed through sanity and disgust till they rediscovered him unreclaimable. Yesterday he awoke to ache, and the primitive terror snagged him: he remembered himself. Suddenly self-conscious, his mind had come to dwell on the horribly material abstract. He had visions. Nothing elaborate; he had just taken to looking more closely, so that when he'd come upon the boy kneeling to smash a frozen puddle with a stone, he'd slowed enough to see him scrape a severed breast, blue bloody glob, into the hole. The vision was religious. Alone as every snowflake, wind whipped and mobbing, he conceived martyrdom, atonement, sacrifice. It seemed to freeze would be an honest death. So he shot himself in the foot and fell, and they went on singing. He decided he was very good at dying. He had spoken as needed

through the years of the campaigns, but did not notice that he
had ceased to think in words until they came back to him now.
Death: big white pigeon of a word floating through the silvered
snow. He was born to it. He didn't make a sound till the last
boot had stamped past, the last wagon ground away, the last
verse faded. Then he babbled: "Abolution, absolution . . ."
Words streamed, bumped, jockeyed for dominion. Words
he'd never heard prevailed: "Ablubultion, bullymunion, do-
predatic, datic, whob." Once he'd been a forester with dreams
of the sea. Now he knew he'd write a dictionary of ecstatic
ultimatum—every instant a new word. His foot burned as he
froze. He said, "I am the victor vanquor conquished."

He died giggling. **Q**

The Men Who Wanted to Be President

Jonathan studied the newspapers for current events. He was so good at it that his teacher assigned him to give a daily report to the class for extra credit. Jonathan proudly displayed his knowledge of complex political issues to his usually confused schoolmates. Most of them didn't get past reading the comics or showing off to their parents by reciting the headlines and the weather. But every morning Jonathan studied all the news. Today, he was studying the attack on an Iranian plane, absorbed in the details of who was right and who was wrong. He stared at the photo of the bodies in the water and read the editorials that argued for each side. Money was to be offered to the families, and Jonathan wasn't sure if this was a good idea. Who would get the money? Where would it come from? How much? Maybe they should offer the families the chance to come live in the United States, and their children could come to Jonathan's school. That way they would be as lucky as he was.

Jonathan felt that it was important that he come to the correct conclusion, because his classmates would be listening and the teacher's extra credit might be determined from his opinions. He knew that extra credit was important, and that no one else got it the way he did. But he wasn't sure what extra credit really meant. Maybe it went on the record that his parents kept talking about. He could imagine the record as a giant LP that the teachers listened to every September and added to every June. He knew it was kept in the principal's office behind a door that said RECORDS.

After much thought, Jonathan came to the conclusion that the captain had been right in shooting down the plane, because he must have been very scared, and that's what the President said and Jonathan usually agreed with the President.

The President must know best. That's what Jonathan was going to be one day, the President, so he figured they should be on the same side of most arguments. Jonathan knew you had to be a U.S. citizen, and that was okay, and thirty-five years old, so he had a long time to keep studying. His mother hinted that it wasn't so easy to become President, but his teacher always said that that was what was great about this country, that anyone could become President. Look at F.D.R., he couldn't walk, and J.F.K. had a bad back, and George Washington had wooden teeth. Anyone could be President, and in twenty-five years it would be Jonathan. He knew it would be a hard road—so the earlier he got started, the better. Just to begin with, he was planning to run for class president this year and began thinking about a campaign strategy. Everybody hated the hot lunches, so that seemed to be a good issue.

Of course, Jonathan noticed that there hadn't been any bald Presidents lately; so if he still didn't have hair later on, a wig might be a good idea. He wrote down the telephone number of the Hair Club for Men that advertised on TV and hid it under his mattress. They kept telling Jonathan that he'd have hair in a few years, by the time he got to junior high, but you never could be too sure, and it would be foolish to lose the nomination for lack of a wig. Some of those men on the commercial looked good—maybe not like Presidents, but certainly like congressmen. So no one would ever have to know.

On the days Jonathan went to the hospital, he would bring the newspaper to read. There was the greenhouse effect to keep up with and what it meant to the environment, the strife in the Middle East, the drug crisis, the continuing tensions in South Africa, Central America, the Far East, Northern Ireland, and, most importantly, the upcoming presidential election, for which there were only two candidates left, a Democrat and a Republican. The nurses said they were impressed with Jonathan's wide knowledge, often asking him for explanations while administering the medicine into the tubes in his chest. Jonathan tried to keep reading while they were doing it. He liked to think of his extra credit record getting longer and longer, in a box that kept getting bigger and bigger.

His mom came with him for these visits and would do the crossword when Jonathan was done with that section. For eighteen months, he had been coming every Friday for his medicine. His mother had chosen Friday so that by Monday Jonathan would be up and ready for school again. But Jonathan didn't think this was such a good idea, because the weekends were kind of shot and Sunday was the most important news day. The bad feeling started after dinner on Friday night and didn't go away until Sunday night, and by then Jonathan had so much to catch up on. Sunday's paper was tremendous, filled on every page with so much information.

One of the good things about Friday at the hospital was that a lady came around once saying she was from a special organization that gave wishes to kids who had to come to the hospital a lot, like Jonathan did. George, who always cried, said he wanted to meet Mickey Mouse at Disney World; Barbara wanted to go to the North Pole; Sandy wanted to go home; Jim wanted to go to his doctor's house for dinner; and Jonathan didn't say, because he was too busy reading. But at home it occurred to him what he most wanted, and he found the card the lady had given his mom and called her up.

Jonathan said, "Hello, I'm the boy who didn't know what he wanted, but now I know. I want to meet the men who want to be President."

Every day Jonathan asked his mom if anyone had called and if anyone had written. He kept up on his current events because it would be extra important to show that he was always well informed. Jonathan felt sure that, Democrat or Republican, his school would show the men who wanted to be President his extra credit record if his teacher got it out. So Jonathan tried to collect more and more extra credit and he even thought about trying to play sports.

Then he called up the Hair Club for Men. **Q**

Mercy

I

So here I am, I'm in the dormitory checking out a small rug the Kurds want to trade me for a radio when up comes Fatma with a note. Of course, she won't come close enough to put it in my *hand.* That would be trespassing. She'd rather stand behind the sheet the Kurds have rigged up to curtain off their section from the rest and wait for somebody to see her feet. As if the sheet were a door. As if her voice couldn't carry through the threadbare cloth. But that's how it is here. No partitions from one end of the hall to the next, but everybody's got a trip wire. It's a warning and a dare: *Cross this line and see what happens. . . .*

So I tell them, rising, "Back in a flash, girls," and they stare without expression, lank soldierly unsmiling women with all their teeth and a slow green fire in the eyes that hangs in your retina after you look off. And forget asking why they're here. Other inmates, it's no problem. "I cut a man." "I sell cigarette without permissions." "I am drunk where everybody sees." Ask a Kurd, you might as well petition statuary. Truly, fix them up in war paint, you can set them out to sell cigars.

The message is from the U.S. Consulate in Antalya. The consul himself is in the yard. *Had a chat with L.,* it says. *Do drop down, Carson. This is good.*

L.. I love it. Like we're in school here, passing notes. Like if we get *coy* enough, maybe somebody somewhere'll take an interest. So I give Fatma two Roach Motels plus a couple of non-dairy creamers for her pains and a nice clean Band-Aid for a sore on her thumb, but then she wants a Band-Aid for the other thumb to balance out, and a third to tape shut her blouse where a button's missing near the throat.

"The Prophet looks with favor on the humbly grateful," I say in my bad Turkish, aiming for a note of fond reproof.

"Pig eater," she says cheerfully. "Hippie demon whore. May your blood turn to piss inside you. May your womb grow hard like a gourd."

Still, she's not a bad little kid, and when I head down to the yard, she follows, skipping. She loves the consul. All the kids do. They can't get over him. The snowy hair, the ears like Buddha, the comedy of wingtips. (Smell the polish! See the tiny holes punched starrily into the hard brown leather!) I call him Agha, though his real name is H. Finch McGuffie. How old is he? A hint: he *says* he can remember seeing T. E. Lawrence fall off a camel. Says that took some doing, falling off . . . When I find him in the yard, he's on the long stone bench behind the fountain, dozing, briefcase for a pillow, book open on his face against the noonday glare. The book jacket is a picture of a fair-faced woman on horseback looking very glowy and above-it-all in long desert robes, while down below a bunch of Arabs romp and frolic in the sand, waving guns.

"It's a biography of Lady Hester Stanhope," Agha says. "Do you want to take a crack at it?"

"I thought you were asleep."

He pulls away the book and props up on his elbows. The bambini who were plucking at his laces break like birds.

"Those well-turned heads, timeless faces," he sighs.

"Who's Lady Stanhope?"

"Nineteenth-century Englishwoman who ran away to Lebanon to live among the Druse. She found herself a castle on a mountain and declared herself queen. It worked, too. They worshipped her."

"Suckers."

He holds it out. "Try it. You can tell me how it ends."

God love the dude. Will I read it? Probably not, but he won't rest until it's in my bag. My Santa Claus, my pal.

The first time I met Agha was in winter, the day they brought me in. I was in the *kogus* testing cots (the *kogus* being what they call the ten-bunk section of the women's jail reserved for foreign nasties like myself) when a message comes: some high-up type is waiting for me in the yard.

I figured Interpol. They want more stuff on Sky. Sky's my man, my num-buh one. Four years ago we met in Heathrow. I was on my way to see my new boss, a widower, an anesthesiologist with three young sons. I was going to be the American *au pair* girl. I would wear flat shoes like Mary Poppins and favor all his brats with equal measures of strictness and forbearance, and I would *not* disgrace the agency that landed me this job. I would be pert. I would be boyless. I would turn myself around. And when Casanova with the demon smile and the Rastaman Vibrations sweatshirt offered to help me with my bag, I would say *no,* of course, but absolutely *not,* no fucking *way,* when he led me to the ticket stand for Air Jamaica, because, as he put it, *everybody knows London licks the bone in March, so let's be nice and let this mystery come down, because as Bob Marley has so rightly put it, who feels it knows it—and I know you feel it because I feel it, and how could I feel it if I didn't feel it from you?*

I was fifteen then. Turned sixteen in Nevis, seventeen in Crete, eighteen in Stamboul. Sometimes I think about that anesthesiologist, all alone in Heathrow, everybody streaming past. The agency had given me a photograph: small worried man with thinning hair. Sky's hair is big and sunny, it flops like peonies. He wears a harlequin jumpsuit, track shoes, and a small gold earring he stole off his mother, which brings us to the next thing:

Sky has had his extralegal moments. Still, if he did one fraction of the shit they tried to lay on him, he'd be a millionaire, or crazy, or just dead.

So that first day in jail, when I learned about my fancy-schmancy, only-here-to-help-you visitor, I thought, Thank you and fuck you, *signores federales:* I pass. Then there was another note, and another, and finally I went down. And it wasn't Interpol at all. It was someone else entirely. And the way his white hair stood up around his head in one stiff swirl, he looked like Mr. Softee, like meringues.

My consul. Agharoonee. Agha-waggah-woo.

He told me the picnic basket's from his wife, Grace. The berries in the muffins were handpicked. I could expect to see him twice a week, he said. What mail I would get would come through him, and not to worry: diplomatic pouch gets left pretty much alone. As for the guards, no problem there, either. They know him. He's been visiting this jail since 1966, and not just to see Americans. There was a Swedish girl, and before her, an Israeli, two gals from Salzburg, a Finn . . . The Israeli was a vegetarian. Was I? No? Good. And relax about the trial. Piece of cake: they do dearly love to scare you, but they always let you off in the end. What was it, anyway? Six grams of hashish? Ten? No matter. Almost certainly I'd be in Iowa eating turkey with the folks within two weeks.

It's Ohio, I told him. And Mom is dead. As for my father, I got that piano off my back when I was fourteen, and if it's all the same to you, I'd like to keep it off.

Dear me, said Agha.

Dear nothing. He was a prick, I said.

Agha didn't miss a beat. Well, somebody will be there to meet you. I'll see to that. I always do, he said.

I told him: Just see I get out.

That was Christmas, the trial was in March, and now it's coming on July. Piece of cake, my ass, boy. A nickel and a dime they gave me. Fifteen years.

The bambini see it first. They whisper, giggling.

"It's your pants," I tell him as we move across the yard toward some loose-jointed chairs in the shade. "You sat on goat turds."

"Oh shoot." He cranes around. "Oh, ticks and chiggers."

Chickens scatter when I take my seat. Agha, scowling, plucks his pants and tells me to go inside his briefcase, where

I'll find my mail along with other things I asked for, which is a farce, because at this point I don't ask for anything. Nowhere to *put* it: the *kogus* is already hip high in effects. Towel rack, methane fridge, ice chest, posters, folding bamboo screen, and about a zillion books on Asia Minor—and that's only what I got from Agha. Then there are the goodies you pick up on the *in*side in exchange. For English lessons, an embroidered saddlebag. For a Mt. Rushmore poster, a mandolin-type deal called a *saz* . . .

Slowly, slowly, light works through a jar of Grace McGuffie's homemade apricot preserves when I hold it to the sky.

"You guys," I tell him.

"She thought you'd like it."

"I love this stuff."

When I kiss him, Agha's earlobes go baby pink as shells. "You're in luck. It's from her best batch yet," he says.

And there's more. Spam, troop-issue cranberry sauce, batteries, Snow's clam chowder, halvah, nougat, olives, hair conditioner, and salt, plus, in the side pocket, the summer schedule for Voice of America and some crank mail from people who read the thing about Americans in foreign jails on drug charges in *Time*. (Almost a thousand of us as of Christmas 1973, it said. I told Agha, That's as good as a convention. We could hold seminars—how to organize a lice race; what to do with pop-in visits from Mormon missionaries; folk remedies from prisons around the world for athlete's foot, diarrhea . . .)

Agha gazes while I finish packing up. His arms looped low around his knees, he's taking in the show. Woman fixing tea. Someone's brothers, guests, playing the tambouras, shoulders knocking, swapping licks as if this were just some courtyard anywhere. Girl in headcloth using marble chips for jacks . . . There's a lot of old marble in the yard, and on hot days like today, when the sun is high and white, the marble gets a bleached look, big bones strewn around after a feast. Which is only fitting when you consider this used to be a summer place for rich Greek Jews, and quite the spread, too. Agha brought a book once, with photographs. Twilit wedding parties with honeycake and wide bowls of blooms, colored lights between the arches. My favorite shows the balcony above the yard, a basket of exotic fretwork like the bucket of a hot-air balloon, kids spilling over the lacy rail, a girl dangling a gold braid, the boy beside her reaching out his hands with a delighted sly look, as if he'd just let go a nosegay or a hat.

It's still up there, this old balcony, boarded now, just hanging. Make a pretty fair sundeck if you peeled off the roof. (I love sun. I have this skin, I'm quite fortunate, it tans perfectly. Back in the islands, Sky used to take me to a nude beach and arrange me in the tackiest positions: he was obsessed with making sure the sun could get to every inch. Here, don't even think about it. Show an ankle, you're asking to get amputated at the thigh.)

Agha follows up my gaze. "A hazard, that."

"I think it's homey."

"Oh, Carson." I've let myself get *pathologically accustomed* to this place is the problem he sees here. It scares him. He's all in favor of me making myself comfortable, but he worries I'm in danger of forgetting what a *real home* can be. But when I tell how the balcony reminds me of my old treehouse, he lightens up at once.

"I can see you up there, whiling away the long summer afternoons with some wee imaginary friend." He smiles.

Nothing imaginary about it, and they sure as hell weren't *wee,* I think—but why mess with his good mood? Agha has a thing about my blasted kidhood, thinks I left it on a bus somewhere, wants to order me a whole new package. Cheerful, ponytail, titless, ears fashioned specially to receive late-night calls from little friends named Melody and Trish . . .

"That it for mail?" I ask him then. It's a game he plays. Ever since I decided I would tell him the letters in the wrinkly envelopes with the sloping hand are Sky's, well, he brings them, I'll give him this, but when it comes to handing the little devils *over,* amnesia kicks in hard. The fact is, Agha holds Sky to blame for everything since the fall of Rome.

"Mail?" He pulls a frown. "Since you mention it—"

I put the letters in my bookbag with the rest.

"What's the grand total now, dear? Fifty?" he wants to know.

"Sixty-three."

"Prolific, isn't he?" Agha's terribly polite.

"Ay-yup," I say, then look at him, the long, flat fingertips drubbing at his mouth. He always does this when he needs to remember something. It's his sign. "What's up?" I ask him.

He whispers, *"Damn."*

"It'll come to you. It always does."

"It was good, Carson."

"You're scaring it."

He grimaces. "More than good. Important."

"Hold on. I'll distract you."

Because it never fails. All I have to do is get a story going, preferably a story about Sky, and whatever Agha can't remember comes back to him like that. So I tell the consul about Goa, not that I know anything about it, Goa was just this place Sky and I were keen to visit, but I like to think about it sometimes, our crazy plan. We were going to go there right after Antalya, follow the coast road east and hitch up at the border with a band of Kurdish smugglers and trek all down the mountains and eat no meat, just lots of Tang and buttermilk and feta cheese. Then the strangest thing, Goa started disappearing on us. We couldn't find it on the map. One minute it would be there, then it wouldn't.

There is a pause.

"Well really, dear," says Agha.

"Seriously. It would just—go—*away.* The count said—"

"Who?"

"The English kid. I know I told you about this kid. We kept

popping into him, remember? First in the islands, then Istanbul. He came back with us to use the shower in our room and
stayed three days—"

"*Ah,* yes. With the jewelry."

"Just a locket, actually."

Agha nods. "With the picture of his mother in it, or so he
said. But it wasn't, was it? It was someone else."

"Frances Farmer."

He shakes his head. "Poor lad."

"Poor *hah.* Agha, he had dreams about us. And what happened in his dreams was, Sky and I went to Goa and we died,
and when the doctors went inside our skulls for the autopsy,
all they found were these white wisps of smoke going around
in circles."

"Goa, going, gone, eh?" His little joke.

"Agha, I was freaked! I told Sky: Out. I want him out."

"And Sky obliged?"

"Better believe it. Though he could take or leave the count
himself. He thought he was a stitch."

"So off he stole—"

"Stole is right. Sky's flute. My rings. I was wild. I wanted
to go after him, but Sky wouldn't let me. He was scared for me,
I think: my temper. He made me lie down on the bed and do
relaxation exercises while he went out to buy cherries, because
cherries are so yin, you know, they pick me up like that, which
is probably the worst thing about it, my getting busted while
Sky was out being so considerate, and then just the idea of him
coming back to the hotel and seeing all those black vans, and
looking up at our window and knowing that was the police up
there, waiting for him, using me as bait—it had to be the most
bone-lonely feeling in the world, don't you think? Agha? How
we doing? You remember yet?"

No, he confesses. I'm about to remind him of the note he
sent me when he taps my arm.

"Friend of yours?"

She's standing in the tip of Agha's shadow. Pale, hair in corkscrews, could be ten, eleven, I'll ask Fatma later on. Fatma knows all the new kids. This little beauty came Monday, with the whores. Whores always take their kids to prison. It's a good deal: free medicine, hot meals, safe place to play, and no landlords coming by with cops.

"Shall we give her some halvah?" Agha asks.

But it's not halvah she's after. She's here to see his bridge. The bambini love the consul's bridge. They love to watch him work it loose with his tongue, then stick it out and jiggle it like the gag teeth in joke shops. Finally, he obliges. Her face is glowing like a bud when a young woman doing laundry at the far end of the yard calls her away.

"My father used to forget things. Birthdays. Names. He forgot my name for a whole minute once," I recall.

"Good God, Carson, am I that bad?"

I laugh. "Did you ever forget your own kids' names?"

Agha has two sons from his first marriage, a botany professor and an engineer. Good boys, he calls them, though what's boyish about the loaf-shaped men around the Weber in the wallet snapshot is beyond me.

He's thinking. "I'll admit, when Grace and I got married, I was tempted. They weren't very nice about it."

"Tempted is a different deal."

He leans down and pulls a twig out of his shoe where it's tangled in the laces. "Anyway, I failed. They're my sons, after all, and I love them and I miss them. Rather dreadfully, in point of fact." He sighs. "I suppose I'll miss you, too."

"Miss me when?"

His eyes meet mine. Up go his hands and seize his cheeks. His voice is hoarse: "Saints preserve us."

"What?"

"I remember."

"You do?" I stare at him. "What is it? Agh, are you okay?"

The consul's hands fall flat against his thighs. He tells.

. . .

Later, we just sit there, pondering. There isn't much to say. I fix my eyes on Lizzie Borden. Not her real name, of course, but it pertains. A million years ago, she smashed in someone's head with a spice grinder when he tried to steal a cow, and now her term's up and they can't get her to *leave*. As Fatma says, *The man she murders has a son. This is not America. Always somebody is waiting. Always.*

"July fourth," I hear myself intone.

"That's what I heard," he says dully. We're both a little wasted here.

"As in 1974?" I ask.

Agha rubs his eyes. "As in ten days."

Some yards away, Lizzie Borden dribbles water on her seeds. The seeds are planted in a marble urn as wide around as a manhole cover. Three varieties of mint, parsley, lemon balm, and thyme. Her watering can is a Fluffernutter jar I gave her ages back.

"That's not parole. That's amnesty," I say, my own voice distant in my ears.

Not amnesty at all, he says. On this point the judge is most intent. Amnesty implies remorse. This is a swap. And again Agha runs me through the change in policy that would permit across-the-board exchanges between Turkish prisoners abroad and extra-nationals in jail here. In my place, for instance, the Turks will get an illegal alien from Kurdistan who got busted fencing semiprecious stones in Brooklyn. But the swap is a formality, at least for me. Once I'm home, the courts will drop my case at once.

Had a chat with L., Agha had written in his note. I ask what happened.

"To the Kurd? Haven't the foggiest."

"To my judge. What changed his mind?"

"Heavens. Who can tell?"

"Was it Leyla?"

He tries to put me off with something about the U.S.-Turkish drug thing and what grand improvements are in store now that we're cooling down our war on native poppy growers and Turkey's figured out all this chasing after hippies only makes it look more asinine than ever—but that's batshit, as he and I both know.

"It *was* her, wasn't it? It was Leyla."

"Well, you know she's mad for you, Carson," he says.

"She sold him on me. She made a pitch. As if—goddamn." As if I mattered is what I'm thinking, but I don't say so.

And I think about that verb: *to matter*. It's different from *to count*. Matter is a thing. You can kick it, kiss it, stick it in a box. Anyway, you do, you have to deal with it *somehow*. And it strikes me how, if you don't *matter*, maybe you *aren't* matter. Maybe you aren't *real*.

Agha talks about the press. He wants me to be prepared. I'm about to be a symbol! The New Liberalism and all that.

"I'll laugh, I'll cry, I'll kiss the babies—"

"Seriously."

"Consul, I love Turkey. It's like a mother to me. The people are so cool. I cannot wait to come back here. I'm going to lead tours here. Bike tours for teens. We'll do the vineyards, *les grands châteaux . . .*"

He has to go now. Duty calls: a crop of Fulbrights down from Ankara, he's taking them to Pergamon. We rise together and he passes me my bag and finds his own.

"Ten days," I say.

He watches me. "I'll stop by Tuesday. Will you manage?"

"Maybe not."

"Dear girl."

"I can't get over it. That Leyla Van—"

"Carson, if you let on to her I told you—"

"My lips are sealed."

"I mean it. This is supposed to be a secret. If word gets out you know—"

"Please."
"All right. Good."

I I

Four months ago, when Agha said Leyla Van wanted to meet me, I said no way. Some Turkish copper heiress the old man bumps into at an embassy reception with an interest in my case—so what? Then he let fall she was the only niece of the same judge who sent me up. Well. Still, I couldn't get too pumped about it. The trial was over, after all. Said Agh, There's still the outside chance you'll get a pardon. Talk to her. They're close, Carson. This could help. I said, *Right.* He said, Please. I reminded him what the good judge called me in his statement. Riffraff. Scum. Degenerate. In other words, a pardon was not in the stars.

One has to say those things, said Agha, it's a point of pride. This is a hard time for Turkey. You can't know.

So the judge is sending me his niece, I said. How sweet.

He said, You miss the point. The judge doesn't know she wants to see you. Nobody knows. The move is hers alone.

I said, She's slumming. She wants to see the little hippie. She's one of these guys who lives to hate America. I'm a dream come true.

But no, oh no, he cries. She loves America, she is obsessed. Reruns of *Bonanza* on Turkish television are her passion, *ponderosa* the first word she ever learned. She read *Parade* in the USIA libraries. She made a Hula Hoop out of a garden hose. She heard Elvis on the NATO station. She bought yo-yos, teased her hair.

So if this Leyla person is such a groupie, let her go there, I said.

He said, She's scared. She's certain every last American knows about your case, and if they find out she's related to the wicked judge (and here he smiled, quoting), "They will be hosting me a necktie party."

Fuckin-A, I say.

Then come the violins. Agha tells me she's an orphan. He "knows" I'll groove on this. Her parents died when she was seventeen, boating thing; the funeral went on for days. Everybody loved her father, he knew Ataturk, they hunted boars together in the Taurus.

I tell Agha about the time my dad met Jerry Lee Lewis in a bar. They both needed the toilet, but some guy was in there with a girl. Jerry Lee was about ready to kick down the door.

Says Agha, Well, her father—

Forget her father, I break in. What's her damn father got to do with it?

A *wide* pause then.

People's fathers, I say.

Say you'll see her, Carson, he says quietly. Do this thing for me.

I say, Suppose it backfires? Like she wants to talk about world politics. I hate politics.

He says he's thought of that. He already warned her: she was wholly *enchantée.*

I say, Truly. I mean I'm sorry about Vietnam and what's happening to little Laos, but it's not like Mr. Kissinger is going sleepless waiting on my personal opinion.

He says, Never mind Laos. She wants to hear about oh, beautiful for spacious skies, home of the true and the brave.

I remind him. How it's been awhile.

You'll remember.

I say, Like years.

He shrugs. Talk about your childhood, he suggests. What you told me about your piano teacher. Or the time it hailed on your block and all the hailstones came down shaped like Mexican sombreros. Tell the kinds of stories you might suppose a woman who made a Hula Hoop out of a garden hose would want to hear.

And that's what I did. And when I was finished talking about the Mexican sombreros, I told Leyla Van, only niece of founding father Ataturk's good friend, about go-carts. About Chevrolets. Catholic bingo. Nonstick cookware. Wading pools. The Civil War Memorial in City Park. Girl Scouts. Miniature golf. Meeting Al Gibbs under the bleachers at sundown when I was supposed to be detaching beetles from the roses.

And all the time I talked she fixed me with her eyes, her Steve McQueen eyes she called them, after her main movie star. Eyes of such a concentrated blue it chilled me. And everything I said she taped and studied and remembered. She called me her Scheherazade, I called her Memsahib, or sometimes, per request, doll, sugarshack, or hon. Tell me again, she'd say the next week. Tell me what is called your bra.

You mean the over-the-shoulder-boulder-holder?

And once more, the weather stocking.

Not a weather stocking, doll. A wind sock. That's where we went to dance. Out on the municipal runway. We'd throw open the car doors and turn up the radio as loud as it could go and dance for hours. Even in winter. The wind sock made a sound like blisters popping. And cold?

So cold you wept, said Leyla, her blue eyes dancing. And in summer was the monkey house.

Roller rink, I said. Where I hung out with the guys under this picture of a chimp in skates and a baseball suit playing a cornet . . .

And Leyla Van would clap her hands and cry, laughing, Oh, Carzone! It is so tender! So American! Can it be true?

No, I said.

The word she never heard or, if she did, never wanted to believe, because it wasn't long before Leyla Van was coming around as much as Agha—on different days, of course. It was better with the visits scattered out. And she'd say (she loved to say this): Okay, now—*go*. Give me the works. What it was, it was like she was the Queen of England (I mean the *main* one, with the waist like a wrist, and the ruff) and I was her knight-errant, back from the wars and delivering the news.

Hey, Leyla even looked like a queen, the way her domed

forehead popped out like a knee, or a fist, and how she sat straight as a scepter in her high-backed chair. These chairs, along with a small creaking table in between, came from the warden's office. The rest of it, linen napkins, cushion for her back, gilt-rimmed wasp-waisted glasses for the tea, she brought herself. Unreal. All around us in the yard, bright-skirted prostitutes and baby sellers and gypsy racketeers hunker low over bowls of yogurt as if this is nothing but a stop along the highway, a grove of poplars with a long view of the steppes. The dirt is hard, nubbly, mined with trash: an antique Royal typewriter stripped to the chassis, clots of tea leaves like worm castings, bottle caps, bits of peel and bone . . . But does Queenie care? No fear. Her good wool skirt lies so flat and stiff across her lap it could be a writing board. Her hands are on the writing board, her exalted gaze is on my mouth; I jive, she glows, I jive some more . . .

Jive so much, sometimes, lights are coming on in rooms inside my head I didn't know were *up* there—and it takes me back to school, when I first discovered jive for real. The one I told about an eyeball I found floating in a bowl of lime Jell-O, the one about my mother's dying words *(Au revoir, Jean-Phillippe* was what I told the world she said—as if Mom had time for words: she was choking on a piece of *fish).* And those were just the throwaways, the message-in-a-bottle lies; you toss them out and see where they wash up, and if they don't, no problem. A good lie, on the other hand, was like travel-ing. It had its own true itinerary. Like a magic carpet, it got you places, took you *out.* Took you to the movies, into clubs, fraternities, motels . . . I mean, I *loved* my lies. I had a gift.

Sky loved them, too. When I think of all the stuff he used to make me tell him when he got turned around inside his head in Tunis, or Saint Kitts. All the crazy nights he couldn't sleep, couldn't even shut his eyes . . . He'd say, Tell me about normal folks. Folks with *consoles.* With the big turning globe in the library that opens up into a bar, two crystal decanters and a flock of glasses in a velvet nest. Tell me about *this.*

So I told. And it was a marvel how they came to me, all those long golden stories out of nowhere, stories he could lie back in, stories that curled up around him like a canoe and took him all the way to where it got light again and he said I saved his life . . .

Not that Leyla needed it like that. Not that I knew *what* she needed. All I knew about her were the tidbits Agha fed me: older husband off on business six months out of five. Son in school in Berne. Seaside villa outside Bodrum. Pheasants. Greenhouse. Cooks. Then, what I could see myself: fine threads (and never the same outfit twice), a fussy manicure that matched her mouth, that gemlike stare . . . So Queenie is lonely, I decided. (Only, don't lonely people yap your ear off?) So she needs a conversation piece to toss around at parties. (Only, wouldn't she have quit coming after visit three?)

Finally, I accepted it. Agh was right. Reason not the need, the lady had a thing about America that went on like space, and that's all there was to it. She was possessed. The stories eased her, took an edge off. They were like—fairy tales! That's how she heard them. I really *was* her Scheherazade, only instead of laying down a line about scimitars and djinns and girls with rubies in their belly buttons and long silky veils, I talked double cheeseburgers, Top Forty, foosball. Because that's what Queenie liked, laugh tracks, up stuff, no doom and gloom, no mystic woe. Keep it mild, keep it easy, keep it nice. Which was fine, mostly, until after the fourth or fifth visit, and I started wondering just when the hell these free tutorials would start paying off.

She's using me, I told Agha.

Well, you're using her. Fair's fair, he said. Besides, she's Turkish.

So?

So Turks don't suffer favors lightly.

.Tell me how she suffers, I said, smirking.

Still, when she came, I talked.

III

I should have been asleep. If I'd been sleeping, I'd've slept on through it like everybody else. As it was, I was thinking about the minaret outside the window near my cot, how black it looked, like a long, wet, pointy-headed needle poking up, one of those cured-in-cobra-venom death sticks some sleepy geek in a loincloth is always stepping on just before the hero rounds the bend (Major Duckey, sir? *Do* come quick, sir! It's Komombo, sir! I'm afraid he's got himself into a bit of a *spot,* sir!), and it occurred to me, you know, how it's always some Komombo, some toiling moon-faced butterfingered extra with a wife and kids we never get to see, never even *think* about, because after all, it's Just Komombo, except of course nobody is Just Komombo when you think hard about it, which is exactly what I'm doing, when all at once they're here, in the *kogus,* four guys with something on a stretcher I can't even tell is human the way they tip it, not lifting it, just kind of tilting it in the approximate direction of the cot nearest mine, the way you might shake a bone into a dog dish, like this was scraps, is what I'm saying.

Pros.

Then they're gone. Shazam. Like a movie running back-ward, they slip out the same way they come in, past the *kogus,* past the trashed-out section nobody lives in I call the Bermuda Triangle, past the whores' enclave and the six slumbering Kurds . . .

And I'm lying under one of Agha's L. L. Bean all-cotton cast-off sheets, and I am seeing this, and I am thinking, Jesus Christ in the foothills, is this not the way? Seven months I'm all alone here, nobody to play with from one end of the week to the next except a washed-up consul and a Turkish house-wife with a crush on Steve McQueen, and *now* they start con-sidering my social life? Ten days before I leave?

"Lordy, Lordy," I say softly. "Look at you."

No answer.

"Speak English?"

Not a peep.

So I go over to her, right? Thin face with nose to match, dark hair, longish, a single spear of silver shooting back from the brow, long hands. She could be French, Italian, even Greek. Not likely, though: her ears aren't pierced and there's no mascara. Clothes aren't giving anything away, either. The sandals are the kind you see anywhere from Delhi to Caracas, blouse a button-down generic, the cardigan a snoozy gray. No information in the shalwars either. Lots of tourists buy them ready-made in the bazaars. They think wearing peasant pants will endear them to the host culture and win bargains.

"You okay?"

Silence.

"Hey. I'm talking here. You want a Coke or something?"

She's awake, all right. No question. The eyes on mine don't stir.

"How about hot chocolate? Courtesy U.S. AID." I smile, rising, tell her more while I prime the Coleman, where the *kogus* starts and ends and why it matters, and why it's not a good idea to go poking into the Bermuda Triangle, although it looks benign enough, nothing but a lot of junked sinks and busted cots in between my section and the rest. Still, there's a vibration there, strange things have been known to happen . . . And about nudity: no way. The Finnish girl here before me set off a riot when she tried going topless. Seriously, they almost turned her into second base.

Is roomie listening? That black-lit stare tells me nothing, but I go on anyway: "And something else that takes getting used to. How the food works. You can always buy your own. Vendors from outside come every day with glass-walled carts full of *kofte*, shish, all kinds of eggplant. So you get bored sometimes, but you don't starve. As for the screws, not every Turkish guard is like you see in the movies, with the nose out to here and the weird degenerate intentions. There is a new guy, Oktay, he does needlework and still labors under the illusion he has a job to do, so stay away, but Ali's cool. You can hit him up for quilts. And Memed'll read your chicken bones and the Laz'll knit you beautiful long socks with leather soles in exchange for a couple cans of albacore tuna . . ."

I'm rambling, but I can't help myself. "Just don't go thinking you can go to them for *help* is the thing. You're on your own here. You make the good times and the bad times both. It's a responsibility! The whole trip is up to you, which is mostly an advantage. You can write, sleep, fart around in the yard, sing along with the muezzins, read your mail, which, Agha, that is, Mr. McGuffie (he's the consul here in southeastern Turkey) brings twice a week. He does his best to see nobody dicks with it, but anything can happen, so I keep mine in a rucksack I drew all over with these evil eyes, and I'm here to tell you, nobody goes near that sucker. It's better than a bomb."

Hot milk bubbles on the flame. I stir in cocoa and walk a full mug over to her cot. Crouch low.

"So what's your name?"

No answer.

"I'm Carson."

Not a word.

"Isn't that a weird name for a girl? My father picked it. It was the name of the roadhouse where he took my mother on their first date and he felt a need to honor it. So first there was a Carson the parakeet, who died, wouldn't you know it, of a chest cold the night I was conceived. Then there was a puppy Carson (Dad found it in a sand trap at the country club where he had this job once doing the grounds), but it took off and got mashed up somewhere. Then there was me."

There's a glitter in the eyes now. Very small, sharp, like pins. I grin. "I used to plead with him: Take me to Carson's Happi Shak. I wanna go to Carson's. I was on his back about it as long as I could remember. He never did."

When her lips move, I dip in: "Say what?"

"I know you," she says.

"So you *are* American. I knew it."

She looks at the mug between my hands, the pale cocoa level with the brim, shuts her eyes, rolls over. I put the mug beside the cot leg. It'll be there for her when she wakes up.

It's not true what I told her. I went to Carson's once. Middle of the night. This was right after my mom died, I was thirteen, my father came out to the treehouse and yelled up, Put some clothes on, angel. We're going for a ride.

I wasn't keen to go. Angel was his pet name for my mom. He was drunk.

It's a school night, I answer finally.

At this he laughs. Big fucking deal, he replies.

So we're driving on this stupid road and the whole time he never once quits singing, some nappy-headed blues his friend Howard Perky taught him: *How can I love you when you're treatin' me so mean . . . You're my daily thought and my nightly dream . . .*

He pulls off the county road into a parking lot, kills the lights. The building in front of us is dark and low, boards across the windows, a lone bulb in a wire mitt above a metal door scarred over with a z-shaped line of rust. I say, It's closed, Dad. But when he gets out, I join him. At a planked-up window he has me sit on his shoulders so I can find a crack to look through near the top. Then he passes up a match.

Light up, he says. Then tell me what you see.

I say, Nothing.

He says, Something.

Put me down, I say, shaking now.

Just tell me, Carson. Don't be a pain, he says to this.

Okay, I say. Bodies.

Bodies.

Not whole ones, I say. In pieces. Now, would you please just put me down? Then I kick him in the armpits, hard.

You've got a twisted little mind, you know that, Carson? says my father musingly.

And now I'm crying. I say, You asked.

Yeah, he says. You let the bullshit walk right in.

I'll jump, I say.

Listen to me now, he says. You're wishing it was me that died. Okay. What can I tell you? You wish it, I wish it; believe me, if she had the chance, she'd wish it, too. But she's gone, and there is nothing nice to say about it. She's over now. She's done with. The thing we loved is clay. Are you listening? Inside these drunken ravings are the black seeds of fucking wisdom. You could learn things.

When I jab the match into the side of his neck, he turns, lurching, then gets me by the arms and flips me out over his head so I come down hard and skin a knee.

You burnt me, he says peevishly.

I endeavor to explain. You make me sick, I tell him.

His hand high on his neck, he says, You burnt your ever-lovin' pappy. Then turns to the building to find a window where he can look in for himself, and I go to the car.

And I can just quit snuffling, says my father, driving home. It isn't what I think. They aren't *bodies,* that dim corner jumble of arms and legs and whatall. They're fake, made of rubber, prosthetic devices they're called, for people who lose their limbs in wars and car wrecks and all like that. If he'd known they'd turned Carson's Happi Shak into a damn warehouse, he never would have taken me, he says.

And he doesn't sound so drunk, he just seems wiped. He knows he's fucked up beautifully. Fact of the matter, Mister Dad has been fucking up for months. Carson-raising was the wife's department, and when she died like that, so all at once, it was like, oh shit, what have we *here?* Am I supposed to fix the child lunch? Do I have to meet her boyfriends? Is she going to make me take her into stores?

He couldn't find his stride. One night it was *coq au vin* by

candlelight, next evening pretzels from the bag. You never
knew! Looking at me addled him. Once, he mixed a pitcher of
piña coladas and later on mistook me for *her*. Not fun, believe
me, but I made a clean getaway. Soon as he collapsed on one
side of my bed (blubbering my mother's name like a whiny
little kid), I slipped out the other side and shot down to the
couch. Come morning, naturally, he'd forgotten, thank God.
I mean, I know this is the kind of incident that's supposed to
ruin you for life, but for me it was Just Another Thing He
Botched. Not that I was sorry—I mean, *God*.

But it was just so typical.

Like the candlelight and pretzels.

Like a midnight joyride to a warehouse full of pros-thet-ic
dee-vices.

I mean, for a second there, I thought this was something
that could happen to me. Like if I didn't watch my step, I could
wind up in club-size pieces with nobody to remember when I
was all one thing. I could wind up this kind of *meat* thing.

He apologized eventually. It was the first time ever, and
the last.

Well, to cop a phrase: big fucking deal.

I V

The name of my new jailmate is Ivy Glover. And that's
it. That's all the consul knows.

"All?" I say. "That's all?"

Yesterday, they whitewashed the high wall that divides the
north end of the yard from the little mosque next door, and
already large flakes of cheap paint are sifting down on the
rucksack on the ground between us. The consul picks them off
and shakes them in his hand distractedly, like dice.

"All day long she sits there like a bump on a pickle, won't
say boo, won't even lift her head. Except to say, *I know you.*
This she'll tell me. Every morning, like Big Ben," I say.

"Poor girl," he murmurs.

"Poor her? I'm the one who sets her up with towels, books,

Cashmere Bouquet. Who cooks for her, lays out her clothes."

"Heaven help her," he says sadly.

"Oh, pul-lease."

"She's tired, Carson."

"She."

Agha takes some tea. "Let's talk about your future."

"Shit."

"Do you have any notion what you'll do?"

"You're the consul. Don't you care about her some?"

Another pause and I observe, really notice for the first time today, just how bad he looks, how plain worn down. The rings around his eyes are puffed and bloodless. The hair, that milky aristocratic swirl, sticks out around his head in uncombed spikes like the gonzo scientist in the movies.

And: No, now that I mention it, he doesn't care especially. "No need for me to care," says Agha flatly. "She has advocates enough. Who I care about is you." Then he asks me if I've thought about who's going to meet me when I get to Dulles.

"What advocates?" I ask.

"Carson, isn't there anyone you'd like to be there when you get home? Don't forget, I have a WATS line."

I'm inking in the creases in my palm with a pink felt pen. The sun line, Via Lascivia, lines of destiny and wealth . . .

"How about your pen pal?" Agha watches me. "Sky."

"While Interpol's still on his ass?"

He ponders. "Could Sky send a friend?"

"What friend?" My whole palm is webbed with ink.

"Please stop that."

I let the pen slip to the ground. "Do I have advocates?"

"Nice," he says, retrieving it.

"Agha, she is in my home."

"Not a home, dear. A jail." His cheeks give off a baggy flutter when he pushes out air. "Must I remind you?"

"What's her deal? Drugs?"

"Does it matter?"

"I am asking you. I want to know."

And so it bounces, back and forth, forth and back, until finally it leaks out, or some of it, what dribs and drabs Agha's gathered at the club. No, it's not drugs. It's politics. Ivy Glover is an observer. She does fieldwork for a human-rights outfit out of London. Not Amnesty, but close. Turkey is the latest in a string of assignments in the Near East; she and her husband—they're a team—touched down last week to interview a Kurdish trade union organizer, only he up and died before they got to see him, and instead of taking a plain hint and heading off to the next job, they moped around like softball players after a rain-out and made (and here I quote) "a damn nuisance of themselves"—at which point I cut Agha off.

"Meaning?"

"Who knows? This one belongs to the State Department, and they aren't giving me a thing."

"But what is it she did?"

"Dear, don't wheedle. I don't know."

And he sounds so weary it occurs to me he might be telling me the truth.

"How about the guy?"

"Flown back to the States on Friday. His case was less sticky, evidently."

I let out a length of breath. "Human rights."

"Not your favorite crowd."

"I loathe those fuckers."

"I didn't want to tell," says Agha sullenly.

"The way they iced me when you asked them for support. They wouldn't touch me. I was shit on a stick."

"Well, it doesn't matter now."

I quote, remembering: "While we extend our every sympathy to Carson North, our feeling is that involvement in a case of this nature could compromise our mandate. Assholes."

Agha clocks my glance at the window near the balcony with distress. "Well, don't blame Miss Glover."

"Human rights. Whose rights? Help *me?* Help some no-count hippie-dippie sleaze when there are state-of-the-art heroes to be saved? Where's the sex? Where's that creamy moral rush?"

"Oh, do be still, Carson."

"Starfuckers."

He pushes himself up from the knees, wincing, an old man full of aches.

"Sometimes," he sighs.

"You know what, Agh?"

"I'm listening."

"Life licks the bone."

For a moment he just stands there, brushing creases from his pants, but it's like trying to smooth the rumples out of last week's lettuce, and for once, when he takes off, I am relieved.

V

Here's a story never made it into my weekly talks with Memsahib Van.

Once, when Sky and I were lying on a beach in Siphnos, drinking ouzo from a rusty old canteen, under stars, he starts explaining about triage. I know what triage is, I tell him. Do we have to talk about it now? A lot of doctors playing God, choosing who gets to live, who gets to die, it's sickening.

Not just doctors, he says. Everyone. All the time. Soldiers, bankers, mayors, farmers.

I scoot down his side until my cheek's in the long, cool scoop below his ribs. Not you, I say. Not me.

He snickers. You and me everlastingly, he says.

And in his belly I can feel the cold dark shapes of the words he doesn't say, the edges of them knocking up against each other, like an engine starting, working up.

I ask him, What's in your head, Sky? But he's not listening, he's up on his elbows now, he's staring out to sea.

Carson, he says. Carson, there's a shark out there. Right out there. I can smell it.

I believe him. Sky had a power, he could smell anything—

roadblocks, cancer, rats in the sugarcane, my period three days before it comes. He always knew, too, when I was thinking about my father: he said my skin took on a smell like rain coming, mixed with grass.

There, he says. Right where the moonlight hits the second roll of breakers. Follow my finger. That's where it is. And what it smells like . . . He pauses, frowning: It smells like skid marks.

I watch him stand. He says the shark is after something: he thinks he smells that, too. Next to him, still sitting, I cup my palms and blow inside. There is a warm whiff of supper: licorice, garlic, and sardines; then this handful of other smells, the minty breeze, the village at our back, the surf. This is my breath, my life: it lives inside. I don't have to plead with it, I don't have to do a thing. It's in there, always, holding fast, a small fish resting in a river, hardly even visible below the mottled silver of the river's wild-running skin, this fine exquisite thing of mine, happy, unafraid to feel its firm shape against the water, pushing, filling up its slot with its hard self, *mattering.*

And I remember how I got up then and pushed the word out of my mouth like blowing out a bad seed: Triage.

What? he murmurs, staring out.

Well, fuck, I say.

He points out: Car, it's feeding. It's got something.

He's not listening, but still I talk. I tell him how it seems to me that once you let yourself start thinking in those terms, which life is more worthy, yours or mine or Martin Luther King's, well, where's it going to stop? I say, You think like this, it could get to be a habit, and all at once you're capable of— anything. Where's the humble? Where's the good? Where's the motherfucking mercy?

Come on, lovely, whispers Sky.

He's talking to the shark now.

Stay with it now, he tells it. Easy does it. There.

V I

Thursday is my day for Leyla. She comes at two, not a nanosecond more or less. Sitting in a chair in the corner of the yard where they keep sandbags, I watch her thread her cool practiced way through the goats and the garbage and the abandoned typewriter, past the women squatting on their shins, and the kids. Look at her, I think. For all she cares, they could be potted palms in a hotel. She's so . . . *superb.*

"Carzone!"

"Hey, doll. Have a seat."

She signals the guard for tea. Flaps a cloth across the table while I sit grinning, pats it flat. In the center goes the tape machine, a gilt-rimmed glass on either side, and then the box, tin. She lifts it wide.

"And something special I prepare last night. Do you recognize?"

"Bread, is it? Some kind of . . . loaf?"

"Rice Krispies bar." She beams.

"Ah. Silly *moi.*"

"Next week I undertake the jellyroll. Then the Coca-Cola cake, and the turtles. Do you enjoy a yen for these?"

Which bewilders me, because she knows this is the last time she'll see me. Then I remember: *She* knows, but she doesn't know that *I* know. I'm supposed to think these dreamy assignations will go on in perpetuity. Foxy lady! I'm impressed.

Oktay serves the tea. Spills a little when he sets it down. Leyla stiffens, glowering when he slopes off.

"See the disapproval. A Turkish lady coming here. I make him sick."

"Come on. He's just klutzy."

"No. This is a message. I am a bad person." Her smile is taut. "Well, maybe I am. They will never frighten me away. They make me—guffaw."

All the man did was splash a little tea, I think, sopping up the mess with a napkin from the tin, but that's Queen Leyla. She loves to play the martyr. As if this is facing down the hounds of hell here, some doof spilling seven drops of tea on her new manicure.

• "Relax about it, Leyla. Oktay don't know shit from apple butter. Really. He's new."

"I gross him up."

"He doesn't even see you. He's too homesick. He just got sent here from the military prison at Diyarbakir. All those political prisoners to play with. Never a dull moment. Next to that, this place must look like summer camp."

She cocks her head inquiringly.

"You don't know summer camp?"

"Never."

When I tell her summer camp is where you get to learn nature and fall in love with your counselor and get so good at filching Moon Pies out of other campers' care packages they never know what's missing, she leans across the tape machine and hits Record.

"Tell."

"I knew you'd pull this."

"Come. We have a story," she implores.

"I haven't thought about that place in years."

"Tell about the counselor," she says.

"Oh, Lordy. *Her?*"

"She was a friend to you?"

I'm laughing. "She was a basket case is what she was."

"Wait. I check the sound."

"You really want to hear this?"

Leyla ups the volume, settles back. Smooths her skirt and folds her hands. "Okay—" she says (the magic words), "okay, now—*go.*"

Yvette.

Of course, it's not her real name. She wouldn't tell us this, she hated it. She wouldn't let us tell her *our* names, either. Too much memory work, she said. Who had the time? Instead, she gave us each a number. I was One. I made her bed. Two dusted the little bulbs around her makeup mirror. Three did her nails. And so on. Right where the chore wheel was supposed to hang on the inside of the door, she put a Goldfinger poster of the naked lady, the one painted gold all over. *Me in five years,* she told us. *You wait.*

God alone knows why she took the job. I guess it beat staying home, wherever home was, and as camp jobs go, it wasn't bad. We had a small, warm, squishy-bottomed lake and a softball diamond and a tent for arts and crafts, and if the interstate cut directly through the woods behind our cabin and you could always hear a truck whining, or a cop giving chase to some poor slob who missed the speed trap in the firs, so what? What did we know about those fancy camps up in the boonies with the live-in tennis pro and shrink? We went to Camp Ted Smith. Keds and cutoffs were our uniforms, and if our first counselor wasn't the hippest thing on wheels (a real Save the Negro type, hair parted down the middle, her idea of a hot time was to sit around reading *Sing Out!*), she was more than manageable.

Then she got mono and we got Yvette.

A celebutante. That's what she was. This was her stated goal. Never came to a campfire, never led a hike. And all that stuff they're supposed to teach you about First Aid and how to make some-mores and play the spoons and the Autoharp and jacks—forget it. *This* is what she taught us: how to suck your cheeks in and pucker out your lips like the girls in *Elle.* (You should see us in the logbook, puckering and sucking. We look as if we're about to puke.) And more: how to tell an epidermal cyst from a blackhead, why Moon Drops mascara was the best, how to get your nipples centered in your bra . . .

Other campers were always getting read to: Edgar Allan Poe, Bob Dylan's liner notes, Robert Frost. Not us. The only thing I ever saw Yvette read was an ancient copy of *Peter Pan,* and a wide-open palm. She told Three, All your dreams will go kerblooey. If I were you, I'd throw myself under a fast-moving truck. Seven was advised to stay away from a man in a hairpiece with a teardrop tattooed under his right eye. *My* palm, she just shook her head. Boy oh boy oh boy, she said.

But let me tell you about the bat.

Camp was full of bats. At dusk, you sat outside the mess hall and watched them flicker into life, black-magic hankies out of nowhere. Six, who understood this stuff, said we had to love them because they ate the bugs that would otherwise be eating us, but this was Six for you. Quaker, bones like a bird, very strict and pure, every day a letter from the folks, every day a letter back. We all got letters, Yvette too, but it was no big deal. Yvette never even opened hers. She turned them into hats. That drove Six nuts. It made her just so sad. Whereas Yvette, for her part, thought Six was just great. So, tell me, Six, she'd ask her bluntly, without malice, what's it like to be a closed circuit? Because to Yvette, being good was like being hemophiliac or Japanese. A condition you were stuck with—nothing to be done.

But about this bat—I was on the toilet when I saw it. Hanging off the clothes hook, it looked just as neat and tidy as a small brown envelope. I thought of yelling for Yvette, then remembered she was down at the office, meeting with the director. Clarabelle, that's what we called him, I forget precisely why. He was a big pink smiling guy who played Taps on the accordion and wore socks up to his knees. We indulged him—we felt sorry for him. Long ago, his wife and baby girl died in a fire, so Clarabelle (in Real Life a rhetoric instructor at a junior college) bought Camp Ted Smith to draw himself out of his cocoon, and we knew that if it wasn't for the pleasure of our company, he'd take rat poison and drop dead.

But I'm off the track here. The bat.

When Six gets me by the arm, the broom is in my hand.

Back off, twinkie, I say.

It's scareder of you than you are of it, she says, boringly.

I say, Forget it. It dies now.

Then the others jumble in: Don't use the broom. Use the plunger. Forget the plunger. Throw a book. Don't use that. That's my *diary*.

We're still arguing about how to handle it when Yvette gets back from her meeting. Before we even see her, she marches over, plucks the bat, and flips it in the wastebasket like she's picking plums, flops a towel over it, and stalks away. Of course, we follow. She pauses at the door.

What is this? she says. *Make Way for Ducklings*? The party's over. Go to bed.

But it's hopeless. The wind is blowing rounds from the boys' camp across the lake into our bunk, "Scotland's Burning," shit like that, plus there is this other sound, thuddy and irregular, like a wet sock knocking in a dryer.

I'm the first to get out of my cot. The others follow.

On the upside-down wastebasket at the far end of the porch Yvette watches us assemble, her open purse on one knee, the little jar of nail polish on the other.

Fuckheads, she says morosely. Get back in there.

Six says, That noise.

What noise?

In the wastebasket, Six says.

Then we all look down at the wastebasket, which has begun to tremble faintly, like a kettle on full boil, and Yvette goes, Ahh! You mean her? You mean the sugarplum fairy? Old Tinker Bell herself?

You'll hurt it, Six says. Just like the sheriff in the movies when he tries to get the gunslinger to drop the gun. It's not right, Six says.

Talk about a party animal, Yvette says, yawns. This Tinker Bell can burn all night. A model for celebutantes all over.

You're high, says Six. You reek.

Then Yvette gets up and shocks us all. She gives the wastebasket a kick that sends it soaring up across the grass into brambles. And someone points and someone else yells, *Look.*

Pink! The bat is pink! Yvette has painted it with nail polish. And not just any pink, but a pink so hot, so luminous, so outright *rude*, it makes the rest of that sweet-smelling piny night go all at once as dull as dishwater. Like a debutante's corsage on a faded housedress, that's how this amazing Day-Glo bat shows up against that plain gray air. Flicks up into the trees, ties a neon bow around a sycamore, and disappears.

Check it out, Three says. Two whispers, Tinker Bell! Come back! Eight wants to set up food. Rolos. Milk Duds.

Then Six chimes in her sour chord: Poor thing.

I snap, Poor nothing. This is great.

It's done for. It's as good as dead, she says.

I tell her to shut up or I'll rearrange her bones, although I know she's right, she's always right: she's *good.* Screw her. Somewhere up there a bat is glowing, lighting up the sky. What a wonder. What a gift.

I look for Yvette, thinking, Let's do another. We'll bait the rafters, do a green one, then a red . . . But I can't see her anywhere, she's gone. Vanished. After a while, we go back in, and this time sleep comes fast.

So there's a story about the counselor. I'll tell you one more and that's it. Why would I want to tell you this? Only because it happened that same night, so it seems somehow related, though it isn't, really. Anyway, here goes.

So I wake up and Yvette is packing up her duffel. Time is after three. In goes the makeup mirror, the *Peter Pan,* the mascara. Then she changes into civvies. Fishnets, black vinyl miniskirt, spandex top. I sit up and cross my arms across my oversize T-shirt. I'm the only one awake; she's got to see me, but not till the duffel's zipped will she crack a wink.

Come on, she whispers. I'll show you something good.

So I slip some thongs on and go out after her. What is it? I ask her.

Take the duffel, she whispers. You'll see.

Did he fire you? I whisper back, more curious than shocked. No question our Yvette is flat out the worst counselor that ever lived.

Just take it, okay? she says. I'd help you, but I don't want to get all sweaty.

Then we're winding through the black stringy pines to the lake, and she signals me to put down the duffel on a saddle of grass between the humped-up rowboats and the upside-down Grumman canoes, which I remember looked especially alive that night, all silvery and sleek and bellied up under the high round moon. We go down the wheezy dock together. Then, at the lifeguard tower, she says climb up for the view.

As if a view is necessary, as if it isn't there in front of my own nose.

It's the old canoe from the mess hall, the one Thoreau wrote about, Commander Happy's pride and joy. Indians made it. It's historical. A ceremonial birchbark war canoe, there's a framed painting of it in the Smithsonian, and here it is in front of me, bobbing like a bar of Ivory, and as if that isn't news enough, Yvette has plugged it up with dolls.

There's a law against selling stuff like this to kids, I say.

She explains: friend of hers works in this store.

I say, Ah hah.

He sent the pump, too, she says.

Some store, I say. Some friend.

Because I know you can't get these anywhere. These kind of dolls, you blow them up. Girl-size, right? And they've got hair and tits and slits and Cum-On lips and everything, and scrambled up in the canoe in these *positions,* feet up here, heads down there . . .

What do you think? she asks. You think it'll catch his eye?

Clarabelle? He'll seize a piston, I assure her.

The hard part was lugging the canoe down from the mess hall, she says.

I regard her. Yvette, I say, I thought you liked him. You used to like him. He likes *you.*

She sighs. I don't know. It's different now, she says.

What is?

Him. He's changed. When she sees me stare, she laughs. Dummy, she says. Did you think I got to skip those stupid campfires all for nothing?

I catch up with her when she steps off the dock onto the grass. I say, Hold on.

She hands me the duffel. Hey. I knew what I was in for from Day One, she says, and winks. Shit happens.

Well, I do not know where to go with this. *Shit happens.* What a dreary fucking point of view. I mean, how sloppy can you get? I take the duffel and walk beside her past the mess hall and the archery range until we reach the county road. Then she asks me, How far's Chicago, anyway?

Well, I don't know how fucking far. Far, I tell her. Then I ask her, I say, Yvette. Just tell me. If this was going on from the beginning, how come you didn't leave?

I'm leaving now, aren't I? she says absently.

I mean, how come you stayed at all? I ask.

She seems surprised. It's nice here, she says. The food, the scenery, everybody in the bunk—people take good care of you. She paused. Even he was nice at first. I mean, in his *way.*

And then?

Then he got bored. She shrugs.

And now we're both staring through the trees at the still, black water and the canoe that leans across it like a bone.

Nothing boring about that, I manage dully.

She smiles then. She mutters, Thanks.

A truck is coming, but whether it's the one that takes her out of there, or whether she winds up waiting for a bus, I can't tell you: I don't wait. And when I find the path to the cabin, I don't look back once.

Leyla taps the Off button on the tape deck, then Eject.

The cassette pops up like toast. She slices me a hunk of the Rice Krispies bar and plunks it on a cloth napkin near my tea.

She sips. "Poor child. To be so alone so young."

"Listen, pal. Shit happens if you let it happen."

"She is confuse."

"To put it nicely."

"People are so sad," she sighs. "What's wrong?"

"This tea tastes like hay."

"I ask the guard to bring a Nescafé."

"I'm sick of Nescafé."

She's puzzled now. What's the matter with Scheherazade?

"Carzone," she says hesitantly, "when I'm at university, I know girls like this. They start out wild, you think for sure they will be lost, then in twenty years you see them and they are fat and happy and all they want to talk about is babies and Italian shoes. Believe."

Across the yard, Oktay gets up from his corner chair and wanders over to the kids. They're playing with the typewriter. Gypsies. It's a mock-interrogation. One girl pecks away at the missing keyboard while a second shakes her fist and curses out a third, who sits glumly on a stone stump and stares at her feet. Nearby, water trickles off the ends of Lizzie Borden's fingers into the urn in quick light-catching drops.

"That guard again. The one who hates me," Leyla says.

"It's cool. He's knows they're just horsing around. He's smiling."

"Hah! *Comme un lézard* his smile."

"They're kids."

A moment later, I lean back. "Jesus. What's he doing?"

Leyla's voice is flat and low. "He is beating up a typewriter. As you can see as well as me."

"He's crazy."

"From first I see him, I know is trouble coming," she observes.

"Bastard."

"I'm telling you, Carzone. He wishes to provide a lesson

to me. Then he will go to his friends and tell them see how I make her run away.''

Each time Oktay cracks down the painted club against the typewriter, little bits of wood break off the end of it and fly into the air like sparks.

"Leyla, he isn't even looking at you."

She smirks. "See her run, he want to say. See how I scare the rich fancy lady intellectual."

All around us, women and their kids are heading for the open arches at the sides, one noiseless stream, like rainwater sliding for the gutters, until Leyla Van and I are the last ones left—plus the other guards, of course, still on their stools, observing, and the maniacal Oktay, and the little gardener Lizzie Borden, who has seen exactly none of this and continues clucking at her new buds as if they were pet chicks.

"Leyla," I say, "I think you have it wrong."

She lifts her chin and smiles. "At king-size risk I come to visit my Scheherazade. My family is determining I am deranged upside the head! How may I run now? I have no fright. Carzone, be brave!"

Like sitting on our duffs while some psychopath attacks a kid's toy with a wooden stick is going to win us Purple Hearts here. Right. Meantime, the typewriter jerks around as if it were a live thing trying to yank free of him. He likes that. Aye-yup, we're having lots of fun.

"I love my country," Leyla reports.

"Great. I'm thrilled."

"I do, Carzone! I wish to love it always. But sometimes it is so hard. Especially when I come here. It is a test for me, this place. Believe."

The club's a stump. Oktay wipes his face against his shoulder and plucks his shirtfront.

"In a way," she muses, "I consider myself extremely lucky. It is the jumbo challenge of my life."

"Wonderful."

Oktay picks up the typewriter and straightens, grimacing.

Sees tiny stone-deaf Lizzie Borden bent like a claw above her urn. When he ambles over, she blinks up, smiling. The man is panting, his armpits stained, the heat comes off him out to here. Lizzie Borden takes the Fluffernutter jar in her two hands and gestures: *Drink*. Oktay bows, returns the smile. Up up up he lifts the typewriter above the urn, lets it crash down hard.

"See how he mocks me?" Leyla hisses.

"You?"

She doesn't hear. She's still leaning in, that moony glitter high in her eyes, showing everybody what a keeper she is, what a tough tamale, what a cowboy, and it strikes me, here's this person, she's so rich and classy, such a soshe, and who in plain truth is Leyla Van? She's another dumb Komombo, just like me. Up to her elbows in the quicksand of her own dispensability, and it's killing her, she can't stand it, she's going to drive herself insane.

So join the club, lady, I think grimly. *If you don't matter, maybe you aren't matter.* But damn if I don't reach out and take her pretty hand despite myself.

Meantime, Oktay leaves Lizzie Borden where he found her, hands around the Fluffernutter jar, blinking down at her ruined garden. Is she crying? Her gaze drifts past me, slow as dust. She looks baffled, as if she's trying to remember something. No, she's not crying. I'm crying. I don't know why. It's not as if he hit the lady. She's so gone she wouldn't know the difference anyway. It's just all of a sudden I'm missing things. A house, a bureau. I don't know. Dessert plates. Friends.

Then it's over. The women return to their cookfires, voices low, impassive, close. They've seen this picture show before. *Shit happens.* Leyla starts to pack her bag. She's bent so low across the table I can see right through her shirt to the back strap of her bra, one of those maximum-security productions like my mother used to wear, with underwire and side-bones and cups like catcher's mitts, or nose cones . . .

My face hurts. I stand and turn. I don't need Leyla seeing this. Fix my watery regard on a salamander, vivid as an orange peel against the dead gray dirt. It jumps its length. Again. Paint squirting. It's climbing up the sandbags. Then I see her.

The observer. Ivy Glover. She's up there sitting just in back of where we have our chairs, slumped against the sandbags as if they were a throne of silk cushions. She stares down at me through weary eyes, does not return my smile. She wants to see what's coming next. She's waiting.

"Carzone, take your sweets. It is for you."

I turn, and Leyla puts the Rice Krispies bar, wrapped up now, in my hand.

"But see! You're shaking."

"Battle fatigue," I say.

"Poor Scheherazade."

Here's how out of it I am: when Leyla goes, I hardly notice. And this could be the last time I ever see her, this could be it, yet all I want to do is turn back to Our Lady of the Sandbags and match my eyes against that hard-blinking face once more.

Gone. Nothing where Ivy Glover sat but a shadow lounging in a long, curving dent along the top of the sandbags, and of course what I remember: the smile that is less a smile than a way to hold the mouth, a form to pour it in. And those eyes. Where did Ivy Glover learn about the eyes? Because it isn't something that comes naturally, that dead-lit stare. Like all great tricks, you have to work at it. How to turn your eyes into two places in your face that just happen to look good above the cheeks. How to turn yourself into your own mugshot. How to suck the light back inside your eyes until there's nothing showing but two dumb balls of tissue, and then, how to *hold* it, make it *last,* so when the man comes knocking for an explanation, he can be looking right at you and still be thinking no one's home—well, it's hard. It takes it out of you. You do it long enough, shit happens. Truly. I know.

VII

Riot in the dormitory. First since March. What happens, a gypsy tries to steal the shortwave I gave the Kurds, and when the Kurds get done with her, the place goes ape. Not that anybody gives two hoots what happens to a gypsy, but a chance to whip Kurdish ass is never to be missed. These sorry Kurds. Someday I'm going to have to get the inside dope on them, read a book or something. *Something*. Get enlightened!

Way down at the far end of the dorm, I can see only so much, and, since I know the worst of it will never reach back here, I find some earplugs and settle into bed. I'd offer up a pair to Ivy Glover if I thought she'd use them, but look at her: pots are bouncing off the walls, babies wailing, people getting trashed, and she's sitting on her cot, gazing out, cross-legged, my new kilim tugged cozily around her shoulders as if this is Saturday cartoons.

I turn over, shut my eyes . . .

Two more days. That's what I'm thinking. Two more days and these fireworks will be for real. Agha says you have to see it to believe it. All over Turkey, from the Baptist missions and the NATO stations and the Hiltons and the digs, from the oil rigs and the World Bank offices and the bazaars, Americans come streaming into the port town of Antalya to see the Sixth Fleet light up the stars. *You'll hear so much English, you'll think you're already home,* said Agha, who's so hot for me to feel *at home* it hurts.

Pond scum are the only words for how this pillow smells. I dig out my earplugs and flop over on my side. Then I stand.

"What are you doing?"

She's still sitting, gazing out, but naked to the waist.

"If anybody sees you—"

"Where are the guards?" Ivy Glover asks.

"Never mind the guards."

"They ought to be here. It's the law," she says.

I say, "Do tell."

She clocks me with an absent look. "Then they won't come up at all?"

"Hey, give a guy a break, these are very busy boys. They work a long, tough day."

She rises slowly, the kilim hanging off her hips in deep pointing folds. "Well, isn't that ducky," she says softly.

"Please sit down. They'll see you're naked and get offended and it's dangerous."

"You're funny," she says, staring out.

"Not right now, I'm not. I'm scared to death."

"They won't hurt you," she says mildly. "They're fond of you. It's nice." She looks at me. "Well, isn't it?"

"I don't know."

"Yes," she says. "You're happy here. You've got your little visitors, your routines. You're good at this. I'm impressed." Then she laughs. "Of course, it's not like Camp Ted Smith, with your own private fan club to wait on you hand and foot, but we can't have it all, can we?"

"Very funny."

"No," she says. "You're funny. Not me. I'm like Six. I'm *good*. But filling a canoe with inflatable dolls." She shakes her head. "That was you, wasn't it? You *are* the fabulous Yvette?"

I toss her my blue robe. "Put it on, please."

"But tell me. Am I right?"

"Just do it."

"I usually am about these things," she says mildly, and drapes the robe over her arm. "And I'll tell you something else. You need to cultivate another hobby. Write some letters. Read these books. Improve yourself. Instead, you play the court jester for crazy Turkish socialites. I'm mystified. I really am."

"If you mean Leyla Van, that crazy socialite's the main reason I'm getting out of here," I tell her.

"Is it?" she asks distractedly, staring past me at the smoke. It hangs in the air in folds and pleats, greasy, like wax paper, while just past it, shadows spurt up the far walls and tag the joists. An insistent, bitter smell: molten plastic. I look for people, but the view is blocked by cots thrown up on their sides.

"You're quite sure the guards won't come," she says.

"Be glad. They'd make it worse."

The kilim slithers to the floor. She's naked now. Full loamy hips below, and higher, boyish tits that ride lean and close as muscles when Ivy Glover lifts her arms up into a long, tall stretch.

"Lady, what are you doing?"

I follow her around the *kogus,* past the ice chests and the towel rack and the desk. When she continues on toward the Bermuda Triangle, I stop.

"You're asking for it."

"You realize we've met before," says Ivy Glover then.

"They use rocks," I say.

She tests the mattress of an empty cot. "It was on a beach," she says, stepping up. "Jamaica."

"Please."

She muses on: "It was a small sunny private beach, and all the people there were very pretty. Then there was you." She holds up her arms. "You weren't pretty. You were beautiful."

Kids see her first. Then some more. It's starting now.

"The man you were with," she says. "Good-looking fella in a jumpsuit, right? Who didn't care for the way you were developing your tan?" She laughs. "My God, the way he kept *recomposing* you, like something on a spit. He had the whole beach watching. Don't move, he'd shout. Stop fidgeting. You'll ruin everything!"

"Nothing you can say—" I start. She clips me with a laugh.

"And still you held your smile," she says. "Your lovely witless terrifying smile."

The women gather quietly, eyes slipping down the pale length of her, blankets pulled so tight around their shoulders you'd think this was the dead of winter and we were in the woods somewhere clumped close against the snow. Here's the egg lady, there the girl who made Agha show his dentures. The kid who played the Grand Inquisitor in the skit with the old typewriter. The one who traded me a saddle blanket for a pair of fake-fur slippers. The ring they make around us could fit comfortably inside a small schoolyard.

Fatma shuffles forward first. Ten years old and worried as a mother, she whispers, "Carson."

I say, "Yes." I say, "I know. I know. I know."

"Tell her she can't do this."

"She doesn't understand." Fatma sees my finger wheeling at my ear and translates for the rest. The muttering that follows her remarks is low and anxious. Good luck or ill, madness—Yankee madness in particular—is never merely neutral. Meanwhile, I am trying not to stare at that spriggy palmful between Ivy Glover's legs. I am trying not to think what I am thinking: *Mine used to look like that. Before I came here, mine used to be as thick as grass. So thick Sky once said he'd like to scalp it for the remembrance of it . . .*

"I know something else about you," Ivy Glover says.

"Not now," I say.

She says, "I know the man they're going to swap you for."

Fatma takes my sleeve. "What does she says now?"

Ivy Glover smiles. "Not personally, of course. But I heard him. He spoke to a group of us at the UN. Remarkable. Barely spoke above a whisper—he's almost eighty, after all—but what a spellbinder! The case for Kurdish rights was never made with greater love and vigor. I can see why the Turks live in terror—"

"Liar."

Her smile fades. "Sorry?"

"He's a thief."

A long pause then.

"Is that what you were told?"

"That's what I know."

"Life isn't very square with you, is it, Carson?" she says.

Nail her, I tell myself. Just go for it. She'll never know what hit her. And when she's down, you can wrap her up in blankets like a burrito. But when I lunge, she snaps a knee up and pops me on the chin so hard I don't even *remember* reeling backward into the net of arms behind me . . .

Fatma holds my chin. "Carson? I think right now you come with me."

Still on the cot, Ivy Glover is swatting down a swarm of hands. Is she actually smiling?

"You could die, you know," I tell her.

She calls back, "I don't know. Do you suppose? They may rearrange my bones a little. Either way, the point will carry."

Her dark eyes shine.

And then it comes to me. She wants this.

Fatma tugs. "Come now. Come."

"She set us up, Fatma."

"Yes. Okay. We talk later, yes?" She pulls my hand.

"Fatma, she wants this. It's a plan."

The women part as easily as cloth when Fatma steers me through. "See?" she murmurs. "All of us your friend here. Nobody want you to be sad. Carson is a nice lady. She make a pretty home. She nice to the little children. This in here is everywhere well seen. *No* problem."

"She's going to use this, Fatma. She's going to fuck the whole thing up."

"Poor nice Carson," she says, guiding me into a doorway.

I pause, turning. "Will you kill her?"

"Go. Go through. Is better out," she says.

"Kill her. Will you? Would you just do this thing for me?"

"Look." She points past me and I turn around and see where I am. This is the balcony. Somehow, during the riot, somebody got the boards off and pried wide the door.

"All the pretty stars," says Fatma, gesturing around.

I step onto the jutting platform into the wide full night.

"God," I say.

"Moment."

Ten seconds later, Fatma's back with the kilim. She settles it around my shoulders and pushes me into a squat. The stone bricks against the back of my head are cold and she reaches round me to pull the rug up over my head.

"And some water?" I ask, shyly. "I'm so thirsty."

As if I didn't know she'd gone. As if the locked door at my back could keep the sound out. As if that were all it took.

VIII

Another doozy Leyla Van is never going to hear:

Once in the islands, Sky took me to a rasta village in the hills and left me to hang out with the girlfriends and the kids while he took off to do some business with the dreads. I knew when he came back he'd be high as geese and after me to tell him stories—did I mention how he loved my stories? He said I could talk the white off rice. It was my view of things. I didn't mope around with a chip on my shoulder. Things were the way they were, and how they were was how it was. Amazing, he said, how many Americans, women in particular, were unable to absorb this simple truth. The drive to fix it was in them like a hot white stone that never quit glowing. Fix the killing fix the boyfriends fix the mothers fix the world. Swaddle everything in attitudes, positions, mindsets. Swaddle everything to death, because that's what it came down to, love or hate, the same bland smiling murderous aggression, same inability to walk away from it, just leave the fucking thing alone . . . And there was nothing Sky couldn't find a way to leave, I mean leave perfectly, like, say, the way he left his girlfriend-before-me's letters, the coldest shit, any other person wouldn't touch them except with tongs, and then just to whisk them to the trash, but not Sky. He had to read them constantly, as if by repetition they could be neutralized, detoxified, worn down to marks on the page. He had a gift for working up the angle on the thing that released you to see it sheerly, no expectations, no four-year plan, as if you were a palm tree that happened to be standing next to it, or a hydrant, or a shoe.

But anyway, about this village, it was the kind of place Sky creamed over, smack-dab in the overheated center of a gone-to-seed coffee plantation, far away as Mars. Friends said we'd never find it, and when we did, finally, I guess the glory and amazement of our perseverance should have been enough. Should have but was not, and try as I did to keep an eye out for this or that discrete cultural particular—Haile Selassie in a gilded frame, a Lion of Judah decal on the side of a toy Tonka, goat soup evolving in a rusty drum that used to be for boiling cane—I couldn't bring it off. His Imperial Majesty looked bony-faced, bereft. The dung-fed fire stunk up everything, and each time I put my foot down, it was like popcorn how the fleas jumped, not to mention all the dog shit and the spoiling fruit rinds and chunks of dead machinery and, I mean, *so what,* finally, if they grow herb and listen to Bob Marley? Take out the herb and plant opium poppies, it could be a mountain village in northern Laos. Flatten out the hair and cheekbones, it could be some sad-ass Zuñi pueblo in New Mexico. Turn the dial to C & W, a backwoods trailer camp in Maine. Which is all a way of saying, simply, that no matter what your choice of drug, poor is poor and shit is shit the wide world round, and when Sky came bouncing up behind me with a rap full of *buds so fat that just to look at them can get you off, but seriously, babe, these dudes are geniuses, the stuff they're pulling off with cultivars and grafts is past the size of dreaming* . . . I was in no mood. No mood at all.

Sky, look, I said.

He gushed, And something else. I met a monkey.

The baby. And I pointed down.

Cute, he said. But let me hip you to this monkey, Car. It talked to me. And then it sang. And here's the thing. It sang to me like Fred Astaire.

Hyir him, mahn, said his new best friend, a rasta named Bunny with heavy ram's locks and a steel hook where he'd lost a hand cutting cane. The baldhead hahve a gif', mahn.

I do, you know. It's true, said Sky thoughtfully.

I said, What's it eating, Sky.

A brief respectful pause.

It's dirt, I said.

Bunny gazed down at the baby with an expression of acute

distress, his long pelt swaying as he shook his head. Doan be eatin' on de dirt, mahn, he said.

Hearty appetite, said Sky.

I looked at him while Bunny lilted on: The dirt nuh fe the Rastaman. Percival. Me speakin' to you, mahn. How you gwan mek war on Babylon wit' bellyful of dirt?

Sky crouched, his arms across his knees. Carson, do we know this child? he asked.

He'll get sick, I said.

Something in the face, said Sky.

Rastaman nuh play like so, said Bunny. Rastaman respect de eart'. Nuh *snahck* upon it, mahn. De eart' fe seed. Fe tree and grahsses, mahn. Fe bone of all de martyrs.

Leaning forward, Sky passed a wide palm before the child's grimy face, then yanked it back. Damn, what an aura. It could raise a blister, he said, rising.

De grahss, de seed, de bone, crooned Bunny. Percival. Doan *vex* me, child.

Maybe I'll go back to my father's house, I said.

Him like he mother, mahn, said Bunny. Stiff-neck. Stewpid. Ugly. But is he not an ugly bwoy?

Sensational, said Sky. Takes ugly to a whole new place.

Assuming it's still there, I said.

His mother also vex me, mahn. Sometime when I see her, I so fright I-self I gwan run fe cover.

Assuming the old fuck didn't lose it in a card game, I said. Assuming he would still at this point even *recognize* me.

Sky stretched. Hey, Bun. Got a Red Stripe?

Bunny peered. What mahtter wit' de girlie, mahn? She cryin' up a river.

Sky nodded. It'll pass.

Not that I miss him. How could I miss *him?* I said.

Doan be sad, now, girlie.

Sky dropped his voice. Bunny, did you ever get a tingling where your hand used to be? As if it were still there?

Bunny blinked. All de time, mahn. Come at night, de tingle-tingle, wake me so I jump out of me *skin.*

Well, she's tingling.

Bunny fixed a bleary eye on mine and nodded. Ah.

He got so strange, I tell them between ragged breaths. After she died, he got awful. He wouldn't talk to me. I was this scum, I hear myself explain.

Bunny thinned his eyes. Not smiling, he moved closer, and before I could step back, he raised his hook, plucked a loose strand of hair from off my cheek, and looped it neatly back behind my ear. Then, with his good hand, he pulled a spliff the size of a man's finger out of his shirt pocket and put it in his mouth. When he inhaled, it flared and sputtered like a trick candle.

He said, Come hyir. Shut your eyes.

Sky, I said.

Now push out all you air, he said. Come on, now. Me know you got more air than this.

Bunny held me close, the bare hook resting cold against the back of my neck. He matched his mouth to mine and moved my lips apart with his tongue. He blew in slow. The smoke poured in like water. Then, before I could exhale, he reached his good hand up and pinched my nose and lips, hard.

So you give it time to work, he said gravely.

My eyes were swarming. I thought: *My skull. Somebody, go get my skull. It just came off me. It went into the trees.*

Okay, Bun, said Sky.

It rough. I know it rough, Bunny purred.

My face was streaming. I heard birds. I thought: *Save me. Mama. Father. Dad.*

Hey, good buddy, Sky said. Let this girl live.

I fell down retching when he let me go.

Me only try to help her, said Bunny sullenly.

She knows this, guy. Believe, Sky said.

Why she doan' allow I and I to help her? Pretty little t'ing like she. She prejudice?

It's okay, Bun, Sky said.

What her problem, mahn? It de best herb in de island, mahn. I t'ink maybe bes' in de world.

Bunny, Sky said. Hey. Yo, *Bun.* She understands.

They didn't kill Ivy Glover. They fucked her up, though. They went to work. Fatma clued me in later: how the prisoners got the American in some kind of mild hold and tried to put a sheet on her, but she popped out and smashed some whore's nose, at which point they figured it was okay to quit being so polite and get serious, which is something Turks can get so fast it makes your head spin.

As for the guards, they had a card game going and did not appreciate the interruption, but they lumbered upstairs finally, cranky and inept. From the balcony I had a good view of them laughing and stumbling as they hauled her away with the little bundle of her things in a sack. Another stretcher went out, too, but it was covered. Then some more guards came with walkie-talkies and rounded everybody up and sent them out into the yard to squat in a circle with their hands behind their necks like war prisoners while the guards searched the dorm.

Interesting how long before I realized it was me they were looking for. They figured I'd escaped. They were crazed! Of course, they could have asked. The kids knew where I was. I was right where Fatma put me, propped like a broomstick in the balcony, staring out. I wasn't doing anything. I was just sitting there, considering. It was fairly pleasant, actually.

When the guards found me, finally, they were so grateful I thought they'd kiss my feet. *Why would I run when in a day I'll be as free as you?* I felt like saying. They led me down and had me go into a squat with all the rest. Which is when I saw the smashed urn and wondered how old Lizzie Borden had managed in this fray, and when I learned from Fatma, who was next to me, just who stretcher number two was for.

Which confused me.

Why would anyone go after Lizzie Borden, a little old lady

hardly bigger than a spoon? But they didn't, Fatma said. Long before the riot broke out, she died in her sleep. Just slipped away as peaceful as a saint, and when I learn this I know—never mind there's no connection—the swap is off.

IX

"Not off," Agha assures me. "Postponed. Until the investigation of the riot is complete."

It's July 4 and I am in the yard, standing, studying the urn, while Agha waits for me to join him on the bench, the picnic basket at his feet. It's all the food Grace McGuffie fixed for my release, my freedom feast; the idea was to eat it on Agha's roof while we watched the Sixth Fleet unleash its fireworks. Poor Grace. I can smell the fried chicken and potato salad from over here. Agha said she had the guest room totally repainted, fresh flowers on every sill. He said she's "sick about this. Really."

I consider the remaining seedlings. Oktay did a number, boy. The lemon thyme is past recovery. I think how Lizzie Borden used to water, never pouring directly from the jar but letting the water snap briskly off the ends of her fingers. Dip and flicker, dip and flicker. When I talk to Agha, I don't turn.

"I brought you something. That book on Lady Stanhope. Remember how you asked me to tell you how she winds up?"

"Please come sit," he says.

"Thirty-seven rooms full of cats and garbage. One cup and saucer, and a teapot."

"Carson."

I take a butt out of the mint. "So now you know."

"Carson, I am so sorry."

"It gets worse. The teapot had a busted spout."

"I mean about the swap."

"Oh, that."

"Please, dear. Sit with me."

I do not turn. "Let's talk about Ivy Glover," I say then. "I heard the thing on the BBC. Did she really lose her eye?"

At length he answers. "She'll live."

"What I don't get is how they could have put her in jail in the first place. I mean, if she's so fucking important—"

"Don't curse."

"But I'm so curious! Was it really a big screw-up like the Turks are saying, or did she do something and they just decided to forget about it?"

"Let's just say whatever set it off, it certainly looks like a mistake right now."

"Poor old Turkey."

"I tried warning them," he sighs.

"I remember."

"Let it go, I said. I begged them. This one's—"

I finish for him: "Big."

"Well, not her personally. But what she stands for."

"As opposed, for instance, to what I stand for?"

A silence now. I turn.

"She's good, isn't she? She had a program and she saw it through. She could have died," I say.

He pulls the basket up on the bench and flips it wide.

"Come on, Agh. Don't be small now. She was great. She had the news out before she was even off the plane! Famous human rights activist savagely beaten in provincial Turkish jail in flagrant violation of the international laws providing for the protection of blah blah blah—but forget about *me*, she says. *I'm* still alive. What about the ones who don't have a U.S. passport? What about the *Kurds*?"

"All right, Carson."

"Thousands of them, jillions, in jails all over Turkey, and why? Because some Turkish cop overhears them talking in their own language, probably some insanely treasonous remark like Hi, pass the yak butter, please, or Could you please loan me that recipe for Kurdish cupcakes—"

"Would you settle down, please?"

"And before you know it, all these senators and editors

and college president types are saying: Well, what *about* the Kurds? And: Wait a minute! We're about to send a nice old man back to *that*? We can't do that. That's murder!"

Our eyes meet hard.

"You didn't have to lie, Agha."

He takes a bottle of cherry juice from the hamper and twists the top.

"You told me, you assured me, the guy they were going to trade me in for was a nobody. A common thief."

His eyes on mine are flat as dimes. "What is it, Carson? Are we politicized? Have we found ourselves a cause?" he says after a pause.

"He's not a thief. He's a—hero."

He wipes his mouth, pinched as a wrinkle. He says, "Yours?"

"That's not the point."

"No?" And now he's smiling, a cold slow smile I don't like at all. He says, "How did she do it, Carson? What magic did she work to inspire this sudden show of interest in anything outside your misty little world? *Not*—"

"Agh—"

He clips me off: "—that as an exercise in pathos goes, this one is undeserving. It may interest you to know that Grace and I are more than nominally sympathetic. But, my word, dear! You've been living with your little band of Kurds here for seven months. More than half a year in which to impress your dear Agha with your convictions—"

"They would have killed him."

"Man's got more zip than all of us, my love. I doubt it."

A big beat then.

"You know what? You rather make me ill."

Agha puts the cherry juice on his knee and turns it in his hand. When a pigeon lights on the far end of the bench, he doesn't turn. I join him. Another cherry juice is in the hamper. I drink hard.

"Sky used to bring me this," I say. "Anything with cherries."

"Yes, well," he says tiredly. "Sky's dead."

"I could eat two kilos at a crack."

His voice is dull. "He died in Goa."

"There is no Goa. Check the map. It's gone."

"There is a Goa and he was there and that is where he died. As you know, Carson. As you knew within a fortnight of your arrest. He went there with a boy named Palmer Riddleston and died in his hotel room of unspecified causes. His mother flew to India, identified him, and took the body home. His mother's name is Florence Seeps. Her son's name is Wally. I talked to Mrs. Seeps, Carson. I tracked her down and called her up."

When I put the empty bottle back in the hamper, I see the book with the letter in it.

"How'd you get ahold of this?" I ask.

"Ivy Glover took it by mistake," he says. "Or the guards took it when they packed her things that night. Anyway, it came to the office with the pouch. Your letter, the one from Mrs. Seeps, was in the flap." He pauses. "I read it."

"No shit."

"It was the first time I've ever read anybody else's mail in my life," he says.

"Well, you picked a live one to start with," I say. I mean, what's *this* shit?—have I corrupted him? I flip the book open to the flyleaf. *This book is the private property of Michael H. North* reads the inscription in red crayon. Then, underneath, in a raw sloping scrawl like a grin too shiftless to hold up more than one end at a time, I read: *For Carson, On her 7th birthday.* The book is *Peter Pan.*

"Hi, book," I say. "My dad gave me this. It was his."

"How much do you recall about this Riddleston?" Agha asks. "The one you call the count."

"He got around." I shrug. "Some guys just do."

Agha pulls the book out of my hands and sets it on his knee. "Do you remember telling me about his locket?"

"Maybe. Look, can we give this thing a rest?"

"I think you remember," Agha says. "I think you remember vividly. He had it with him when he stayed with you in Istanbul. And he had it with him, too, when he and Wally Seeps ran off to Goa—"

"I never knew a Wally in my life," I say.

"But he doesn't have it now. Mrs. Florence Seeps has it. And do you know why?"

"I'd like my book back, please."

"Because Wally had it on him when he died."

"Come on, Agha," I say. "Will you give it?"

"Did I say on him? Actually, it was inside him. Among other things. See, Wally's mother authorized an autopsy. She told me on the phone. I don't expect you know that."

"Nobody's named Wally," I say.

"You understand, I don't mean in his stomach."

"I want my book."

"You have your book. You're holding it."

I stare down. "An autopsy." I start to cry. "Oh, God. She didn't write me about that. Oh, Jesus."

After a moment, he pulls the book away from my face and mops me off with a fresh napkin.

"Now, now," he says.

It starts again. "Lord, I'm turning into some kind of *case* here," I hear myself say. I'm crying on his arm now. He doesn't put his arm around me; enough people are staring at us as it is. He just lets me. When I pull away finally, the whole top part of his sleeve is slick with wet.

"Man," I say. "Oh brother."

He takes two unopened envelopes from his vest pocket and sets them on the book.

"These came today. And don't tell me they're from Sky."

"I won't."

He's waiting, though. At length he rises. "Never mind. It's not my business."

"Agha."

He holds a hand up. "Enjoy the chicken. I'll get the hamper Thursday."

"The thing is, I don't read them."

"You don't read them."

"I don't even open them."

A pause.

"Yet I take it you know whom they're from?" he says.

"I have a hunch."

"But as long as you don't open them, you wouldn't want to say for sure. And if you can't say for sure who's writing you, how can you be expected to respond?" His smile is tight. "And yet your pen pal persists."

I shrug. "Some people just can't take a hint."

"Poor Carson. What a burden."

"Too little too late," I say.

He turns his hands into a steeple, slips his chin between the fingers at the top. "Fifty, sixty letters I have watched you tuck into your bag—"

"Sixty-five."

"And that's too little."

"Go home, Agha."

And he does.

x

I saw the count dance once. The same night Sky smelled the shark, we strolled up the beach to this after-hours club we'd heard about, where the smell of herb was thick as fur and de reggae very irie, very roots. It was fun dancing with the jiffypops (what we called the rastas because of how they do their locks, all fat and bouncy in those massive hairnets). They take the music serious. They comprehend the groove.

Then there was the count. Pretty little white boy high on the amp, showing off his dance steps, very Latin, very hyper, very hot. His eyes were jittery and round. Plus he was tootling around on a toy plastic saxophone with colored keys.

De dreads be nuh amuse.

The first bottle hit him in the shin. Second clipped his arm. By the time we got him out of there, his lip was cut and he was bleeding all over my blue halter.

They didn't like me, did they? he said as we walked to his scooter, parked beneath a royal palm. It was my sax-playing. I could tell. Jealous sods. A shame about your smock, dear.

Hey, I said. Shit happens.

He nodded. Charming. Your philosophy of life?

It gets me by.

He looked from me to Sky, who was holding the sax for him and blowing random notes into it, browsing for a tune. He murmured, So I see.

Sky, give Charlie Parker here his sax back.

Keep it, said the count, clambering up onto his scooter. I've seen you two around, he said, smoothing his hair back from the sides. You have a way of sticking out. He smiled at me. Is it love?

We both looked at Sky then, who was playing "Frère Jacques," his head thrown back and his bare neck showing gold against the moonlit dark.

Do you know what he told me when I met him? I recalled. He said, *Behold, I will cause you to ride in high places.* From Isaiah. I laughed, but he wasn't kidding.

Well, how nice it's working out, said the count.

If I worked at love, I wouldn't trust it for a minute.

He got the kickstand and raced the motor. He said, Love you don't have to work at you won't know how to keep.

Do you work at love?

Heavens, no.

And you don't keep it.

Haven't got a place to put it, darling. He fingered his bruised lip. Do you suppose I'll have a scar? I never scar. Even as a boy. It was a problem in a way. People were unkind, he said.

You're full of shit, aren't you? I said.

He took my hand and kissed my palm. I found that saxophone in Spain. See that he takes care of it, he told me. And took off.

The courtyard's empty. A breeze lowers itself down, prowls the corners, kittenish. Plucks my hem, swats around some leaves and bobbles them a little closer.

Agha asked me what I'm waiting for.

What I'm waiting for. It's a question.

A question.

It's my daily thought and my nightly dream.

So what's the difference now? What change is here? Shit *does* happen. Like Goa, people come and go, and sometimes they come again. One day they make a promise, next day it's can't you take a joke, girl? Stars so old we don't even have a number for how old they are can disappear without a trace, oceans dry up overnight, and you're complaining about love?

And *then* they say, Have mercy.

Like it's so easy. You reach into your pocket and pull it out like change: Have mercy. Just . . . *have* it. Like it's just on you, like a bottle of Excedrin. Take two mercies and try to sleep, dear. Take it on the rocks, with lime. Like here's an answer. Like anybody knows.

And here comes a nice new coat, buttoned up over somebody's head so I can't see the face. The coat is dark green and woolly, built for snow, and so big on its new owner that when she wanders over to the bench the long sleeves trawl the dirt. Her voice comes thickly through the cloth:

"Do you like?"

"Hello, Fatma."

"I get from Kurdish terrorist."

"Are you a terrorist today?"

A small hand wriggles through a space between the buttons, mimes a handgun. "Tah tah *tah.*"

AMY GODINE

"You don't look like a terrorist. You look like a mailbox. Is that the story here? You want some mail?"

"Okay."

She squirms until her head pops out between the collar and stares down at the envelope I've put into her hand.

"You don't like it? Here. Pick another."

She peers into the open bookbag and regards me sharply.

"All these is for you?" she says.

"All these."

She picks one up. "But you don't open!"

I smile. "Scary, huh?"

She turns the letter in her hand from front to back, her eyebrows working closely. Holds her tongue between her lips and rips it wide.

"So what's the news?" I ask her.

Heat thumbs up the sides of her small face. "You know I am no reading English, Carson."

"So? Make it up. If it's good, I'll give you Band-Aids."

Her eyes drop down. She tips her head. "Band-Aids with a pencil?" she asks, not looking up.

"You got it."

At length, she makes an opening report: "You is in luck, I think. This from a very famous person. Maybe a movie star?"

"Go on."

"He say he buy a new cow, very nice, pretty, and he loves it very hard. And it make a milk for him, this milk is selling like the hot pancakes, so that's good. But now he got a problem. This pretty cow, it always make him think of you. Every time he see it, he have to think, Where is Carson? And everybody from"—she looks up—"what is your village, please?"

"Ohio."

"Everybody from the Oh-high village is becoming also sad, because where is Carson? And he say, Be nice to Fatma."

"Is that right?"

"Yes. He say, Poor Fatma. She is so tired from all this reading, he say now *you* read. Okay?"

163

"Me?"

"I am sorry. I just tell you what he say."

"And does he say I have to read them all?"

"I think he say this. Yes!"

"Because it's my move now. I'm on the spot here. Because nothing's going to happen out of nowhere. Love takes work."

"For sure!"

"Work and mercy."

"*No* problem!"

"And you really think I'm up to this?"

She takes my father's letter from my hand and puts it in the bookbag with the rest. "Okay?" she says. "Now we go up?"

And so we do. We go up to the *kogus* and I give her Band-Aids and a pencil, and I spread the stack of letters on the desk and take a chair. I also get the reading lamp. Not that I need it yet, but this way when it starts getting dark, I can just keep going—assuming, naturally, it is what I want to do. **Q**

Delivery

Six sexual tips will save your marriage. We thank God every day. Day one: grapefruit. Little Timmy lost an arm. More household hints. Lactose intolerance. My man was cheating on me. God was our co-pilot. Send for directions. Accessories make the difference. My baby needed a kidney transplant. Christmas cookies! Sunscreen. Are you a shopoholic? Here's what's hot. Quick hits that you can cook all in one skillet. Photo inset. Secrets men will not tell you. We needed a medical miracle. Edible flowers. Kicky hats. Eileen needed a makeover. God gave us a sign. The children no one wanted. Step four. Sugar blues. A pit bull bit my baby's face. Clip this coupon. Moisturizer! Here's how to open a closed man. This page. High fiber treats your kids will love. God was in our corner. My hair was a disaster. Baby Billy was drowning. What's your daredevil quotient? Clear mascara. Mammogram. We prayed to God all night. Answers on page 97. Know your skin type. What do men like best in bed? Lipstick tips. The eight-day complex carbohydrate wonder diet. Crib death.

Send us your story. **Q**

Run in Place

She had not been where they had been. But they were
experts in going away and they were taking her with them. It
did not matter where they bore her, through groves of lichee
nut or passion fruit, so long as the red bus with unlashed
windows throbbed on and she was going away. A way trickled
through a valley sown with boulders, melon heads, pocked
with lichens, that toppled into the road, guillotined by the
wind's blade.

The bus tripped on them, stumbled, tore off a red scab,
limped on.

Ida sat behind the driver. She wore spry pantsuits that did
not wrinkle. Her face had all their creases, scored and cross-
hatched, skull-deep. Her next trip was already planned.

"My goodness," she said, "I guess I've only got a last trip
left in me." She laughed. "To the cemetery."

Ida announced the movements of the bus.

"We've stopped!" she called out, as they wavered into a
one-pump gasoline station.

"We're on our way!" she promised when, transfused, they
pulsed strongly back to the road.

Ida's friend sat next to her, repeating and recirculating her
words. "That's right," she said. "On our way," she said.

Creaking, the bus wheezed to a plateau pierced with thorn
trees. Each tree was crowned with a bird, feathers hanging in
charred strips. The coughing bus hacked past the plucked
trees and she saw that beaks buried deep had drawn blood.

Chickie and Deke sat across the aisle from each other,
dividing their harvest. They had bargained in souks and bazaars and from the windows of dhows and trains of grand
vitesse.

"Cindy gets the silver pin," Chickie said.

"Not LuAnn?" asked Deke.

"LuAnn gets the plate and Cindy gets the pin," Chickie insisted.

"And the ring?" Deke wanted to know. "Who gets the ring?"

"Rhonda gets the ring unless she has an attitude," said Chickie. "If Rhonda has an attitude, then LuAnn gets the ring, and we don't give anything to Rhonda until Christmas and then maybe we'll give her the plate."

She saw them drink from their bottles of mineral water like chalices, probably pledging rogation.

Some passengers were sick.

The guide told the driver to stop, motioned with an angry thumb. The passengers shuffled to the little shacks, hunched over, fists to their mouths. The driver, bored, bit into a mango, let its pink juice ooze over his mustache, spit flecks of its pulp when he yawned.

"It's the fruit," Ida told a mother when the woman returned with her gagging child.

"She didn't eat any fruit," the mother said.

"The bugs from the fruit jump into everything," Ida said.

"They sure do," said Ida's friend.

The mother felt her child's forehead—hard enough to smack.

The passengers lurched back to the bus, the guide prodding them to their stalls. The driver twitched his mustache over his scarred teeth, pinched and stroked and tickled the red bus back to life.

"We're moving!" said Ida.

"Moving!" said her friend.

The road branched and branched again, arteries narrowing to capillaries. It was so clogged with rotting skins, spoiled seed, chewed rinds, split pods that the bus could hardly pass. There was a sign, but in an alphabet she did not know. In the distance were black pools which might have been the mouths of caves, or the doors to troglodyte homes, or blood let from a slaughtered animal.

A boy left his family and stood over her, eyes dark as plums. His face was a whole bowl of fruit—red delicious mouth, apricot-flushed fuzzy cheeks, pomegranate kernel teeth.

"Do you have children?" he asked.

She gave herself two boys.

"How old are they? What are their names?"

She gave them ages and names.

"Why aren't they with you? Why are you alone?"

She put one into summer camp, sent the other to stay with a French family. The boy returned to his parents.

The week before she had given herself three daughters. She could not remember their names. From here on she would stock only the alphabet: Alexander, Bridget, Cassandra; Daisy and Esme; Frank, Garth, and Hanna. When she got to Xavier, Yvonne, and Zoe, she would start again.

The bus pitched onto a fragile bridge. A plank was missing and she could see the dark current dripping and sucking, filled with leeches trying to cup themselves to the belly of the red bus. It pitched, shook the suckers off, reached land. Water pursued the vessel as mist, spattering on the windows in drops that seeped into one another like cells under a microscope.

A Swedish couple read thin-skinned books. When the guide spoke they hissed and gargled names and dates they knew he had wrong. Or perhaps they spoke of some other place. She tried to see the titles of the books, but the covers were blank. When the rain clots darkened the bus, the Swedish couple turned on flashlights, slim as glow worms, and kept on reading.

The scrim of mist dissolved. A black curtain muffled the bus in its dusty folds. The curtain lifted, to show a stage bare except for a kiosk lit by a single pear-shaped bulb. Hooded figures, their faces smeared space in their cowls, turned away. A dog with fur sticky from old wounds melted into the wings. The shadows congealed and the bus flowed on, the stained and spotted bandage of the road winding ahead. The curtain sank—putting out the bulb's bloodshot eye.

A couple on their honeymoon sat next to each other without touching, wired into headsets. They jerked to different beats from their separate electrodes, wore matching florid shirts, grew their hair to the same length. The woman sneezed, wiped her eyes.

"Joanie's allergic," the husband announced proudly. "She has these allergies to about everything."

"Everything?" asked one of the Swedes.

"Just about," the young man said.

The sick child whined. "Where are we? When will we get there?"

"We're not there yet!" Ida said.

"Not yet," said her friend.

"I want to stop," moaned the child.

"You swear you didn't eat any fruit?" the mother asked hoarsely. "Even one grape?"

"Deke," Chickie leaned across the aisle, "remember when I was so sick, in Sri Lanka or maybe it was Sion. That was the fruit."

"Right," Deke agreed. "Sick as a dog. In Sri Lanka, or Siena."

"She didn't eat the fruit," the mother said.

The bus spurted ahead, gushed through a tunnel. When it emerged a thin slice of ruddy light had been carved on the horizon from its speed. Panting, the bus spilled over a hill and the sliver grew into a globe.

With a groan and a rattle, the bus sank to its knees.

"We're here!" said Ida.

"Here," came the whispered echo.

The passengers turned and stared at the woman who was alone: the boy with eyes like bruised plums, the pale-lashed Swedes, Joanie's red-rimmed blink, the guide's scornful glare.

She looked out to see where they had taken her, these great travelers, who had trekked and bivouacked and cameled and kayaked and pilgrimaged. She saw her own house, suffused with pips of blood-red light squeezed from the orange sun.

Her own house.

With its blank windows, its narrow groaning door. **Q**

Affair

We were holding hands. I tried slipping her the tongue, but it was no go.

I had a lot of romantic fantasies about my job back then— not so much fantasies as versions of my life which didn't happen to be the way things turned out.

Well, selling books for a very high-quality house was the way it had turned out. And the truth was, I was going to have to sell fifteen or twenty books this particular day, or I'd never make quota by the end of the month. (When I say "sell ten books" or "sell twenty books," you understand, these are orders, not individual books.)

Anyway, the girl said to me, "Can you just sit here all day? Don't you have a boss or something?"

"I'm pretty independent," I said. "I don't stand for it when anybody sticks his nose in my business. Even if it is a person which happens to have hierarchical superiority to myself." (People are generally so beset with personal failures that it's a pain in the ass bothering with them. Like my ex-wife, for instance.)

I got to Larsen's Bookstore. Some other salesman was just leaving. The guy gives me a smile like I might as well forget it, he just got all of the shelf space in the Western Hemisphere.

The phone is ringing. But Paul Buyer (not his real name, you jerk) cannot answer it, of course, because he is on the other phone. I always wanted to pick up one of those phones and say, "Who's this, Doubleday? Well, fuck off, Doubleday!" But I suppose it would be considered unprofessional.

People are always getting themselves all worked up over body language and communication skills, but I don't see the

THE QUARTERLY

point. People have always communicated, and that includes
lying; like even dogs also have communicated for ages. Me, I
think dog piss contains coded stories the dogs tell back and
forth through the ages, like generation after dog generation,
always laughing their dog laughter.

Anyway, Paul Buyer gets off the phone. (Paul Buyer has a
large mole growing behind his ear, which he fingers with anxi-
ety and irritation.)

"Paul," I say with smoothness and friendship overflowing.

"I can't, Michael. Not today."

"Paul, this is Scarsdale," I say, meaning I've come all this
way. (Nobody has much freedom, and nobody has less than a
salesman.)

"Okay," he sighs. "After lunch. But I can only take five or
six at most, and no new writers this time."

I hate this shit. Not that I have a personal thing about
writers, new or old. It's just that I hate this shit.

I have to eat lunch all by myself. I was hoping to get
out of Scarsdale before three P.M. but only after getting Paul
Buyer to take at least eleven books (orders, I told you!) off of
my hands. But instead of going back to Larsen's right away, I
asked for another cup of coffee.

"Hey, I'm in publishing," I say to the girl who is sitting
next to me at the counter. She is one of your typical girls from
a rich town, not a hell of a lot to do, and probably thinking
about sex and clothes all of the time.

"I'm here promoting a book," I say, like she even asked
me something. "It's a new kind of love story." (There is, of
course, no such thing, okay, jerk?)

"Who wrote it?" she says.

"This is only his first book, but it's very sexy," I say.

"I probably never heard of him anyhow," she says.

I wanted to impress her with some inside appreciation, as
if my life had turned out otherwise. "It's a new story, but it's
really based on a very classic idea," I say.

She shrugs. "I don't read so much anyway," she says.

She puffs on an ebony holder into which she has jammed a cigarette at an awkward angle. Her jeans come down to the line just above her ankles. Black pumps with a short heel. It was obvious she could have made something of herself. She could have been a real sex pot.

"There's a guy," I say, "and some other guy, a kind of good-looking and evil guy, and then there is these two very beautiful women. The hero's not very handsome, but he's funny and charming. And he really likes one of the babes. But he's really in love with the other one. Like crazy, you know? So the two babes are almost exactly alike. Same build. Same tits. Same everything. Except one of them is a blonde and the other one is this raven-haired beaut, and dresses very sexy, and this is the one which the hero guy is in love with. The story starts with when the guy has a fight with the babe's father, who is this rich bastard. I mean, you know, the father is against it."

"This sounds like the 'Patty Duke Show,' " she says. "You know, the identical cousins."

(That's how it is when you tell stories to people out loud. Like the old guys, the guys on top of naked mountains, a campfire at night, the Stone Age. People interrupted, then you went on. Sometimes, you leave stuff out on purpose, and you have to say, "Just wait a minute, I'm getting to that." Even if it isn't true. Even if you never will.)

I told her more about the two babes, the blonde and the other one, like about how they used to be friends because they were almost like twins.

"The evil guy is highly good-looking, and he has this way when he smokes. He sucks on his cigarette and he sticks one finger in his eye. Kind of like an intellectual, you know? What happens is he sees this very passionate scene with the sexy girl and the hero guy. So when he gets the chance, he tells her that the hero guy was a coward during the war, which is all lies, as anybody could tell. So this babe is just shit anyway, so she breaks up with the guy, and the guy gets really depressed and wants to win her back, only the dumb fuck doesn't know how."

"How come she couldn't tell they were lies?" this girl interrupts me again.

"This is the point," I say. "You keep trying to tell the guy, 'This one's just as beautiful, and she would be just the same as the other one if she colored her hair a different color.' But nobody really pays any attention to her, except when they need to get their car fixed."

(Ordinarily, you don't tell this much about a book if you want somebody to read it. But I didn't think she was going to buy it, anyway.)

"Then, he realizes that this girl is very beautiful and that he really loves her all along."

I was getting to the end of the story, and I had a good moral lined up too.

"I don't know anybody that didn't break up eventually," the girl says, jerking the cigarette out of the holder and crushing it with her heel.

Then she says, "The seasons are changing." (Women feel that in their hearts. Not like men, who say these things just to kill time.)

Once you lose someone's fundamental confidence, like your wife and kids, you have done something intangible and irrevocable; then you might as well kill yourself. You say, "Love me again or I'll bash my fucking head in."

But we'll never be as sincere as when they say, "The seasons are changing."

"What's your name?" I asked her.

It was some kind of L name. But I immediately forgot. I have trouble with names. But I like L names.

There are signs all over town pointing to a tiny stream, little footpaths, no cars allowed. Like with most affluent communities, Scarsdale is very proud of simple accoutrements like graveyards, Pilgrim churches, duck ponds, and two-hundred-year-old trees.

When she suggested a walk by the stream, I could only imagine one single outcome.

"You must find your job very exciting," (let's call her) Linda said.

"It's very challenging, and I have a lot of freedom," I said, the uttering of which hurt. (I have never experienced freedom from fear.)

I moved my lips to her face again, but she slipped away.

"I like it here," Linda said. "I come here a lot."

I wondered if she meant that in a romantic way, telling me the story of her life.

"What time is it?" she says.

"I have to get going," she says.

"I really have to," she says.

"I can drive you there," I say.

"Oh no," she says. "It would take too long."

"I don't mind," I say. "It isn't every day that I meet this beautiful a person. And what else is freedom for?"

Meanwhile I am thinking that, on the other hand, it would be great. I could see Paul Buyer and then I could pick her up again for dinner and a movie, and I could be back in New York in time for *Star Trek* unless of course the improbable happened.

But then I would have to tell her that I was really just selling books for a living.

The last time I was at the movies in one of these small towns, they showed a short before the feature film, and a middle-aged usherette climbed on stage and stripped down to her Playtex Cross Your Heart Bra and panties. I wish they still showed the newsreel stuff about World War Two.

All this time we are in my car and I have insisted, for some reason that I cannot understand, that I will drive her to Yonkers and wait in the car while she sees Mr. Averton. I can't remember who Mr. Averton is in her life because she told me while I was thinking about laying her, so I can't ask again. Maybe it will come up again in the context, I am hoping.

My feelings for her are like a giant motor making a lot of noise. But there is no heat. You know the machine is working, but you don't know what it's for.

So I am out of Scarsdale early for once. But I will have to return in the morning, unless of course I spend the night in Scarsdale, which would be very convenient. I hate thinking this way, though, because it is opportunistic. People think like this in New York, which is, I am sure, why people are not happy there anymore.

I thought that Linda didn't know a lot about me, and I wanted for her to feel that I was a good and sensitive person.

"I should go home later to feed my dog," I lied.

She says, "There isn't anybody to look after him?"

I say, "Oh, sure there is. My neighbor has a set of keys, and if I call him, he just takes care of things."

"He just does that?" she says.

"Sure," I said.

"I really am attached to that dog," I say, "though sometimes I have trouble expressing my feelings. I have very sentimental feelings about that dog."

We had a wonderful dinner of some stuff, and then I drove her home.

It occurred to me, as she was telling me about Mr. Overton, one of my hands on the wheel and the other groping, that she was admitting that she had always remained faithful to her "boyfriend Ira."

Maybe I should have given her a chance.

I pulled over and turned off the engine instead. I guess she didn't know why. So she just watched me. I had been very polite and unthreatening. But that kind of stuff hadn't gotten me anywhere.

I pulled her head to my lips, and kissed her. Then I pushed her head down to my crotch. She said, "Hey!" which is very general and could be interpreted as simply surprise.

"Quit it," she said.

I kept pushing.

She had a strong neck. It was like a dog pulling on a leash. I didn't care if I had to break her fucking neck. Her nails lashed out like tiny extraterrestrials on my face, and my cheeks were the mysterious red rivers of Mars. Nothing seemed like me at all. I punched her one, a short, painful, ineffective blow right in the chops.

She managed to unhook her seat belt with her one free hand and open the door. She tumbled out of the car head-first, doing some kind of a semi-handstand on the curb with half her body still horizontal in the car. I grabbed her feet and banged her ankles together before shoving her the rest of the way out.

At least now I won't have to tell her the truth about my job.

And that I have never sung with the boys.

And that I have never held a friend to comfort his grief.

And that I have never overheard someone say, "Michael is a real good guy." Q

Only time to pack up and move

The Burning of John Dee's Library

What I love in this book is how its ashes fall
through the luminous trees;
coal beams stagger to their feet
into flames. Smoke plunges into the roof
rising from its floor in one huge gasp.

Townspeople, fearing his magic, stumble
back, catch blue torches, swallow profanities;
the room spits rocks through windows
crackling as they meld into glass.
Weeks later, we turn the page.

The padlock springs like a cricket
caged in his palm. He unties
a few Bibles, slips them into gaps
on shelves with Bruno and the others:
Zoroaster, Mercurius, Francesco Giorgi;

books knowing what it is to burn.
He reads from right to left fire
in God's hands turns all things white.
The more he reads, the less he knows:
bad scribblings uncross themselves;

women inhale their own flames, back away
from stakes in churchyards and pray.
By morning he lies down, mystified,
refreshed. Some nights, he falls
through the blank end of sleep,

wakes exhausted. Lighting a candle
with a wet thumb, he revives the room—
books on books, the long-condemned
imploring a scholar-magus to blow
dust from tombs and read there.

Winter's Apprentice

The praying mantis tilts
its brittle head, serrates a leaf
with its pincers, swallows—
the bead of its brain so taut
there is no thinking back.
It simply moves
like the sound of a tree falling
apart. Leaning down
into its mirrored eye,
we enter the world
it sees. Here is a new order
of wildness, neither hungry
nor mad, a dry rasp,
the afterlife of leaves.

These November nights, wind
rattles the luminous cube
of our house. I see more
of my family when the weather is bad.
Last night my daughter broke
into a fever. She rehearsed
old age, shook the snowing
crystal in her hands.
It was suddenly rare:
a Polish churchyard locked
in a sea-turtle's egg.
She shook it again, firmly,
held the cold glass to her ear.

As the first snow turns black
on the seminary parking lot,

I back my father's blue Ford
through the warmth of its exhaust.
I am a string of occasions
gathered into my father's
memory. My daughter and I
enter St. Thomas Cathedral,
its high pediment a shoreline
suspended over the astonished
tide of fluting and wax.
What we offer the dead
is guesswork, larkspur,
violets: our blessings.
We choose our seats and imagine
the weather, watch daylight
swell on the windows,
the aureoled faces there.
Heaven is a city:
it has its own parks
and cafes, its own stone plaza
under the lemon trees,
its own hospital where the nurses
are slightly kinder and wiser.
And when fathers die there,
they do not look away
from their sons but ascend
to yet another heaven. My daughter
laces her palms together:
Here's the church, here's
the steeple, open the door;
and we are fingers
on God's two human hands.

Under a blue scarf, a woman
prays, her palms leaning
on the mirrors of each other.

Elegy for Weldon Kees

This is the Golden Gate, the abandoned car,
the red mist that sinks after a great storm.
This is the one flame on its stem,
spinning. We cannot know where
your armadillos wandered, why your chorus
drifted flat and quit, how fares
your dear and fatalist parrot Boris.
You of course were wrong: there are
no public endings. Only unfinished,
private things. You floated the smile
of a bather in your good hand—frail,
bright, a denial of seasons. The world,
you said, is always waiting outside
like a bulldog or a sad valise.
To be involved then was to be worldless,
more lost than losing, a sky plunging into the sky.

Anonymous Rhenish Painting

A woman poses between arabesques
of weightless linen, her belly

bulging slightly in the old way
of beauty, cupping the light

in a crescent like the crystal
face on a dead and priceless clock.

Beside her, the jeweled box,
a gift from her jealous father,

its key small as a newborn spider.
Her pubis is polished to an ivory

surface, uncreased, as though
buffed to a single word

in a lost and musical language.
She is hermetic as an egg.

Her deafness is pure. A gold bird
blazes by the window. The boyish

man in a night-cap enters her boudoir
from behind, undisclosed,

thieving shamelessly a long look.
His mouth opens as if to assist

his eyes. In each eye is another
green boudoir, a parallel man

by the rear door. He longs to peel
the paint off his back in broad,

blue strips, to be the small
gold key turning in her vacant gaze;

and if she should come
to life, it is only as the ancient

ribbons curl to her floor,
gathering to themselves like ears.

Katherine's Eye

It's the faithfulness that fools us,
how its fine red vein
slips under the living seam.

When Katherine lost her glass eye
in the deep end of her uncle's pool,
her brothers scouted the blue

floor, excited and horrified,
listening for its tap and roll.
If you find yourself staring now,

half-forgetting, unsure
which is which, you are proof
of the attention it draws

into its glass bowl
like a silvery helix of fish.
We cannot feel how her shade

thickens to the one side,
which half chills
slightly in the winter.

The two move with the parallel ease
of synchronized swimmers.
They are beautiful sisters

who hide whatever differences
they feel. When she looks through
the partial light across her pillow

into her lover's eyes,
her one pupil grows dark
and large as the room itself.

It's been years, and he is still
curious. The glass eye
beckons him from its foreign places

like a postcard of the planet
earth. It's the color
that paradise borrows from our

better days, glass-
blue, a window in the body
that has no other side.

God

She says,
fucking
my face.

What Happened to the Boy

well he was nagging me to know what time was
so off the top of my head I said time is a lady
I told him hide in a hedge at half past moonset
and he'd see her hitching by in a damp fur collar
shriveled heels spiking the turf

he just kept asking me what time was going to give
    him
so I said grab hold of the hem of her dress
I knew her wrinkled hips would shrug off some old
silver feather and he wouldn't go home
    empty-handed
I said boy you won't go home empty-handed

but he just kept on asking me how to slow time
    down
so in the end I said kid put your thumb between
her clammy knees and just trip her into the mud
I said yank away those damp furs till you hear the
    heart skid
and then bite the hell out of her

so I guess that's what happened to the boy

EMMA DONOGHUE

Sea Change

Is that real?
I said, pointing at her diamond ring,
and *Yes,* she said *yes,*
glass is real.

The Consolation

Boethius says that sons are torturers,
quoting Euripides on the happiness
of childless men. Lady Philosophy
very simply answers him: Pleasure brings pain,
presumably the pleasure of copulation,
the pain of childbirth and of rearing children,
especially sons. Boethius had sons,
who never came to visit him in prison,
or were away on business in the East,
or died as boys of something in the water.
Philosophy concludes with her cliché
about the honeybee: how it gives honey,
then leaves a sting to fester in our hearts.
I sit up late in a motel in Memphis
under a night-light reading this while he sleeps.
His breathing isn't anything like bees.
He said if he should wake before I do,
he'd stay there in the dark and wait for me.

The Lost Boy

He reached a hand around my finger
and walked with me down the hill to the bus
by a broad boulevard under aching light.
We stepped inside a house with tinted windows.
Women in bathrobes moved from room to room.
A bus was coming down a corridor.
I left him waiting there and went back out
to sunlight and on up the street,
where I could see a prospect of the city.
The innkeeper's wife ran in from the dining room
and turned around once on her tiny heels.
She saw me from the middle of her turn.
I was explaining how unblameworthy I was,
since all I came for was to find my way
out of this place, nice as it happened to be,
and all I wanted now was a route of egress
by some means through that back wall over there,
so I could take my leave and make my way
back up the hill I had come down earlier,
leaving my mother at the restaurant
with ivory fingers folded on the table.

Theseus on Hippolytus

I loved her when I sired the boy,
but something happened.
Her favors liened into my heart,
so I crapped out.

"I saved your life!" she learned to shout.
Tough shit, I thought.
Was it my dying turned you on?
Then kiss my ghost.

I ducked the service when she died
and cursed my bastard's tears:
Whine in private, stable boy. Love?
Rut your bitch's mares.

That Spring, Those Woods

I came out of the trees above
the hidden spring and listened while
the hounds ran on, still yammering,
convinced the stag kept to the trail,

though he had not. The water poured
over furred stones and fractured sinks
where shadows let sly fish sleep in
peace. When I stooped over to drink,

I heard a woman singing, downstream. Panting and wet with the hunt's
frustrations, I crept along the
bed, against wind, hiding my scent.

It was the god, and she had laid
her bow and skirt aside, and showed
me, unawares, nothing I had
not visioned I would someday know.

Laving herself—those muscled limbs,
that belly and its vertical
smile—she granted *her* ten fingers
a virgin's love; mine, denial.

When I cried out, hands clenched around
my staff and trembling, she feinted
once, then spoke. On my head two horns
sprouted and grew till I whinnied.

On four I sprang into the woods,
rutting handlessly, tree trunks, stones,
until the panicked dogs bounded
my scent, attacked—and I fell, torn

for all those things she had taught me
to find lacking in myself: grief,
untouched breasts surrendering milk,
the white-lipped entry into life.

Arrest

He went down under the gnarled
trees, knees pulled up, sandals off.
While we feared to pray, he slept,
and from his navel Caesar
sprang, senators, subpoenaed
witnesses, all balanced on
the barely swaying scales of
his need for conviction. I
walked into his dream, saw the
way the scales began to rest
in what he believed, not one
gravity or the other,
but both hung in counterpoint
on the uprearing spindle
of his spine. When the troops came,
he woke quickly, the balance
dissolved. In his world or mine?
I aimed to take a head down
with us, but the ill-swung sword
caught only an ear. He knelt,
cradling the disenfranchised
bud, again and yet again,
against the bloodied man's head,
until even the soldiers
wept and my victim cried out,
I hear! Then they took us all
away, him to his rebel's
death, the four of us to bear
testimony to the just
reward of prophets: if love

is true, I preach, then hearing
is restored, and his dark grave
betrays nothing, and nothing
my insensate denials.

Ovid in Paradise

Once I thought I had
career possibilities, and I
stripped and stepped into the baths
as free of inhibitions as any
syphilitic nymph. That

was long ago, just after
the Republic fell and I understood
that the granaries of the Black
Sea held neither perennial
resurrection nor plenty, but rather
the inevitable empty horror
of the harvest. Also

long ago. Now I wade, knee-deep in
the tender bloodbaths of Heaven, content
to be as nameless as any
here, equable, as I hide
my penis from the daily purview
of the martyrs.

The Buddha Meets St. Augustine in Heaven

"No commerce along this Heavenly River.
God, the landlord; God, the tenants.
Surrender, man, your fierce covenants,
your too-just law, your nimble forgiver."

Sousa

Marching doesn't cure anything

except the body's need
to go up and down,
one side over the other,
for a little while.
Same as sex.
Same as war.

My Brother's Pillow

These indelible yellow scrawls, these
palimpsests bearing the same
message at every reinscription:
   "How tenderly I loved you
      when there was no one else."

The Gnostic Apocalypse of St. John

That last hour we sang around
   the sacramental wine,
and all went well until the scoun-
   drel cried, "And let God damn

that one who deifies himself."
   Then we fell—to a man—
mute, disacknowledging the knife
   he tested on his thumb.

It flashed up once only, once down,
   and he began to dance.
We drank the blood that he called wine
   and left, like thieves, no evidence.

JONAH WINTER

Leaves of Absence

A Message from Chong

God is great.
God is good.
This is Chong.

Gods

All bad things come to children.
Even God, the worst of our dreams,
who rattles like a spider through the hedges.

The dark mother rends the day.
She is a whispering of alleyways.
She leaves them at the schoolyard's edge.
Up the block, the grandfather
sits at the south edge of a brown couch,
drinking. The children sob toward him.
I think that God will eat them.
Even now, he scrapes and creaks in the branches,
hungry for the terrible wild blood of children.

The old man, roused to simple endlessness,
rises drunkenly, stumbles down the hall
to bed. He will never hear
the screams of the children, or how that God,
chewing fiercely with black teeth,
struggles at his kitchen door.

ELLIOT RICHMAN

Zen Love Poem

Nothing else existing
but my penis
inside you and
a great blue heron
standing silently
in my heart . . .
the sound of
blood lapping against
its slender dark legs

Children

It is almost as if we were children,
me fat and forty-eight,
you twenty-nine with three kids—
and a husband with a gun collection.

I count the bumps on the areolas
of your 32A breasts—
which are plenty big enough for me.

You tickle the shaft of my penis
like it was a parakeet's neck.
Then you jiggle my balls and laugh.

We've already gone through
the *Joy of Sex,* the *Kamasutra,*
and *Psychopathia Sexualis.* So,
it's simply enough being inside you,
slipping my tongue between your lip and gum.

I don't think we have much in common.
But I don't care. I like the way
you speed through yellow lights
and how your Botticelli hair
feels on my chest.

After we make love, I microwave dinner
and you smoke a joint
in my Cairo ashtray.

I go to loft windows taller than I am
and look at the moon with binoculars.

I see the Moon Rabbit mixing the elixir
of immortality, the bitter drink
that is only for the gods,
while we, on this earth,
children of Eros and dust,
play out our lives in his chalk-colored light.

MICHELLE RHEA

Outliving Sylvia Plath

She forgot to live
long enough
to enjoy her madness.

Nothing Is Enough

Nothing is enough
until death.
Death is enough.

The Gates of Hell

All morning they were lining up. To eat.
Neither they nor the food was ready.
Nothing was prepared. Except the dog,
his tongue hanging down from his mouth,
who followed each soul like a shadow.

Indian Summer

That summer, Charlie drew a cunt
with a black crayon, taught me
how to lick the alphabet.
My mother almost caught us
in her drawers, putting on
the panties and gowns. He slept
in my bed every night after
his parents split. He taught me
how to trust my pouty lips
wrapped around his hairless cock,
tongue sliding across his crack
the way I sealed my letters home
while away at camp. That summer
we rode each other like horses,
fearing Indians in the bushes
along the edge of a bluff.
Then it was over. We cried
at the airport. He promised me
postcards from another world.
When school started up again,
I wanted to show him all
the stamps that I had mounted.

Protocol

It has been months
since anyone
put his hand on the
back of my neck.
Everything spills
over. The tail
of a rat protrudes
from the bend
in the baby's arm.
My friend tells me
he eats air.
Half of what I mean
to say remains
unwritten. Best
ideas come from
brief glances.
Look away fast.

Threnody

I

Into whose womb was she woven?
Out of whose womb did she plunge?
Is this grief that accompanies us
From one town to another?

II

Not long after the other hid scissors in her bed,
Not long after he chose silence,
Not long after the tall place was cut down,
Not long after all crooning ceased,
She thought she too might be unrecognizable.

Thank God her hands reached out to her.
Thank God they were as homely as ever.
Stroking, holding herself.
Her dear old consoling attached hands.

Solace

I know, I know, it's tough.
I know. It's tough. I know.
It's tough. I know it's tough.
I know. I know. It's tough.
I know it's tough. I know

It's tough.

I know.

Junkyard Poem

Love brought me to the heart
of a junkyard near Conors and Mack.
I slammed my pickup truck
through the padlocked gate,
climbed into the flatbed
to rattle my pinball machine,
its Mardi Gras lights winking
off the rusty cheeks of bumpers,
off undercarriages balled up like fists.

I shake its silver hips.
I tap the gay machine.

Cliff Notes

What if those final moments
before death you realize
it was all made up,
that story about Moses
walking under water, Jesus
leaping from stone to stone,

and you lying there, like Gulliver,
strapped down by your ribs?

The Little Richard Story

Nothing is talking to you
in the numbers, in the leaves.
No *mambo mambo* on the wind.
No colored streamers in the skies.
No one has pasted little notes
to you, like kisses.
No Fred, no Ginger,
no sudden bursting
into Stone Age languages.
No angels clustered in the rafters.
No giants sacked out on the stove.

On a day like this,
without the music
of appearances, creatures
could land and you
would not be able to explain
anything to them, not
the fearless industry of
beavers, or why dust bunnies
prefer the dark, not even
how Little Richard
himself came into being.

I always knew I had the
capacity to become naked

I was just sitting out here in Aunt Mayme's art studio, which used to be her beauty shop, and she came out and said, "Crittendens' is on fire," and actually it was their garage that was on fire, but it was making a big enough blaze for three houses, and then everybody in town started coming around, and there were the Crittendens running around in nightgowns and big fuzzy slippers, and most of the town dogs were there. And the happiest person of all was Muke Crittenden, who probably set it, as he just got out of the pen, where he was sent up for arson and theft and mental derangement. The Crittendens live in a kind of buzzards' nest of Insul-Brick and mill sidings just across from Mayme, and all day Mayme's been watching Muke mose around the yard setting fire to piles of leaves and tires, and so at 9:30 the shed/garage/auxiliary buzzards' nest went up. It was a big fire. The Johnsons' dog Suzy was there, and the Creens' shepherds were there, and the volunteer fire department came fairly quickly, and then Gillard Roupe came roaring up in his red pickup; he's a very handsome young black man who breaks horses, and he was mad. I don't know why. I'm not sure what's going on between him and the Crittendens. Some of the men started yelling to get some of the Crittendens' old cars dragged away from the blaze. I guess that's why they called Gillard. He threw some chains around the axle of this tireless car and snaked it out of fire range. It was throwing sparks in rooster tails off the wheel drums as he tore off with it behind his pickup across the pavement on Dougherty Ferry Road. Gillard looked furious. Muke Crittenden was leaping around with his strange pale hair sticking up, in a jean jacket and tall boots, and Verna was wafting about with her two hundred pounds in a huge polyester circus tent, and the fire was lighting up everything all up and down

Dougherty Ferry. The volunteer firemen started shoving the walls in with long poles, to collapse it in on itself, and storms of sparks were blowing over to the river. So the fire died down and most of the people and dogs went home. Bonnie Rapp drove up and said she'd called the sheriff to try to get him to take Muke away before he set somebody else's house on fire and burnt them up in it. So the sheriff came, and of course I had to go out and stand there and listen. Bonnie did a pretty good selling job; as town clerk, she feels responsible for Blackwater. But they couldn't do anything really unless they had evidence. We stood outside Mayme's and tried to listen when the sheriff went over there to talk to them. She kept saying, "Can you hear anything?" and I said no, so we snuck across the street and crept around the side of the Crittenden house and tried to listen. They were all out back there, beside the glowing remnants of the garage, Muke with his pale excitement and tall boots and jailhouse skin and the old lady, Verna, in her circus tent and fuzzy slippers, declaring wildly that they'd all been inside all evening, all the boys, never went outside, that they just noticed the fire when Gillard Roupe came banging on their door and told them. I said, Bonnie, they're going to see us creeping around the side of the house, because the sheriff was starting to search the yard for evidence with his big flashlight, looking for your standard Arsonist's Fire-Starter Kit, and so we fell over each other creeping back to the street, creep creep creep, the old sleuth's crab step, to stand innocently behind the Johnsons' pickup that says MEDUSA AGGREGATES on the side, with a truly gruesome head of Medusa on it, snakes barreling out of her head in scaly cobra coils, just the kind of logo that makes you rush to the phone to call them for some aggregate. Suzy Dog was standing there waiting for some humans, and began to wag herself into seizures as soon as we came creeping around. We kept trying to listen to the conversation between the law and the Crittendens across the street, and then saw that the sheriff was not going to take Muke back to the Do-Rite Hotel, after all. They drove away without him. And drove over to us. Bonnie tried to tell him all over again that the kid was going to set something else afire—he's been setting fires and stealing for most of his pitiful life—and the sheriff said, "Well, the fire department came fast enough," and Bonnie said, "Yeah, that's because his brother Henry is a member of the volunteer fire department," which gave the sheriff some pause. Well, it's 11:30 now and so far no fires yet, but if any of the empty houses in town, or the old Methodist Church, etc., survive torching as long as Muke is in town, it will be because the Sarshal boys have jumped him and beaten him insensible again. What you have here is your basic sociopath. A couple of pickles shy of a quart.

Nettie Becker has two half-grown possums that she raised from babies. We went over there the other night to play cards and Upwords and Scruples, and she brought them out of their cage. Their names are Miss Piggy and Ringtail. They're so cute they look fake. They look like they're made out of fake fur and buttons and patent-leather ears. So everybody sat around and played with these possums for a while. We tried to remove one from Aunt Mayme, but a possum won't hardly let go of anything with all four feet at the same time. You have to get them to wrap that horrible reptilian pink tail around your arm and then peel them loose. They have feet like hands. We got entirely engaged with them, and then Nettie got impatient and yelled, "Well, bring your possums, girls, and let's go shoot some dice!" So we took them over to the table with us and shot dice, and Ringtail sat in Bonnie's lap washing himself and yawning and washing Bonnie's arm and her sleeve, and Bonnie said, "They must think we're crazy, waking them up and making them do laundry," and Miss Piggy clung to the edge of the table, watching the dice fly back and forth, and smirking under her long rat nose. Then we played Missouri Mania and the question was: How long did it take for a round trip from Franklin, Missouri (just across the river here), to Santa Fe in 1850? So that started Jessie Morris talking about

223

how her late husband's great-great-grandfather used to make that particular trip by oxcart. That was Andrew Cole (he was a Cole on his mother's side—Jessie was a Boulware), whose father was Samuel, whose mother was Hannah, who came here in 1819. Nettie made everybody possum Christmas-tree decorations that look like Miss Piggy. Well, here it is 12:30 and Muke Crittenden hasn't set anything on fire yet. I went over and swept and washed windows at Mama's house, and got a real-estate person from Boonville to come and make out a contract and put a sign up. I'll put some carpet down in the bathroom tomorrow, to cover up that busted tile. Lots of memories in that house. I was buying a piece of carpet remnant from Mary Jane Fahrendorf for it and she said, "Well, we never know what will happen in our lives, do we?" I said, No, we don't. She said, "It wasn't meant for us to know," and I said, No, I reckon not. She rang up the $6.00 for the carpet remnant. Well, I better sign off. We had some Christmas here already. Elsie gave me some pecans off her tree. I gave them all some pottery things called Wiggle Warts. Nettie gave me a beret and gloves to match. The Christmas tree is set up in the town square, shining all over with electric lights, in among the black cedars, and Muke sits, no doubt with glittering solstice arsonist eyes, waiting to light up his unfathomable mind. Q

Dear Recreation Director;

Your Fish Fry on Sat. with all those from the Community was such a treat for us Lonely Old Folks here at the Home for the Aged. I love to see so many young nice-looking people having fun in good Christian Fellowship! That old Scripture I John 1:3, that ye also may have Fellowship with us and truly our Fellowship is with the Father and with his ▬▬ Son Jesus Christ, that the "Lady Preacher" read touched my heart but then, my goodness, her prayer! Who does that Lesbian Bitch think she is calling God a woman? If she does not go to Hell for that then my name's Jim!

In His Holy Name,
(Mrs.) Enid J. Crackel

Socrates up to the castle wall and says, Hey, anybody home?

No answer. He waits patiently. Nothing happens. He calls again: Hey!

The wind rushes in his ears. The sky looks a shade darker. Folds his arms and sighs.

Much later, Socrates, seated on a stone, thinks he hears something. It is a whistle, whistling sound. Creens his neck up ramparting and squints. A fuzzy outline of a man in chain leather, pokey metal hat, shifting slowly from side and whistling to himself.

Hey, Socrates in excitement rising. To his feet. Hey!

The little man looks down.

Hey! Can you let me in? I've been walking for centuries all alone in these deserts.

Croon to creen, the guard says, You are Greek?

Yes!

Sorry. No Greeks in the keep.

For heaven's sake, why not? We are perfectly courteous, respect private property, are almost neurotically neat and clean (a lie).

Orders are, sorry.

Well, speak! Please to your master. And how are you today, he'll permit this one exception.

The master is only four years old, says the guard. Six months since the old master died. And upon his standing orders, *No Greeks in the house.* Until he comes of age, I must et cetera, et cetera.

Ah! says Socrates, but don't you see this is the time to listen to the voice of reason? Simple, do it all the time. You this and that and this and follow the path that logic dictates.

Orders. And he disappears.

Whereupon, struck with an idea and never giving up is Socrates. Hup-two, goes to the surrounding villages and tribal enclaves, gathering a small army of followers. Tells the men that inside the castle they will find everything except eking out a harsh existence. Gladly following, the men, and at the appointed, Socrates leads them in a terrific charge and at the castle gate. The defense easily repels and all save Socrates himself are killed. Spends the next several days in a foul humor. Finally, another plan lights. *He is exultant.*

Following which, Socrates goes to the city councils and boards of supervisors of all the surrounding communities and proposes to construct a subway system that will facilitate the growing mass transit problems of the metropolitan area.

Sensibly, a citizen asks: Who will pay?

Piece of dough, says Socrates. At which, boards and councils readily agree to the logical and efficient plan (which could, in fact, facilitate their mass transit problems). Socrates accepts bids and begins work on Saturday.

In two years' time the ribbon-cutting ceremony, at which Socrates is given a plaque honoring his civic-mindedness. Socrates is among the first trainload of riders. Having no special plans at that moment, the riders simply make the journey to the farthest reaches and back again.

Socrates, however, still fully mindful of his scheme. Disembarks at the CASTLE KEEP station, excusing himself on the pretense of *business.* Reaching the top landing of Castle West, Socrates in business fashion huffing toward the food-storage area. En route, he is seen by the winnowy daughters of the previous master, who can spot a Greek and alert the guard. A chase comes next, during which Socrates is cornered in the wing of the castle that serves as the new master's play area. Socrates rushes young sir with the intention of holding him hostage, but a knight lunges at Socrates and forces him bodily to force the young master bodily against the wooden axis acting as the back of the young master's play horse, breaking the young master's back on the axis and ending his life.

Socrates is hurriedly courted on charges of murdering the young master.

In answer to the question Do you deny responsibility for the young master's death? Socrates says: No.

In answer to the question Do you deny that had you not entered the castle in violation of Castle Law, the young master would still be alive? Socrates says: No.

In answer to the question Do you deny that you willfully, premeditatedly, and in full possession of your reasoning faculties assassinated the young master? Socrates says: Yes, I deny that one.

The jury finds Socrates guilty of murder in the second degree but not of murder in the first degree. The punishment for either is death. Socrates is put to death in the gas chamber along with millions of his compatriots. A statue is erected in his honor in the central park of one of the neighboring villages. The sculpture, done by a local New Right Platonist, is a rendering not of Socrates at all but of Samuel Gompers, early American labor union leader and no figure of intellectual history. Socrates objects mildly and reasonably, but is overruled, *res judicata* (and *tabula rasa*), as being justifiably and literally devoid. The sculptor is then himself thrown in prison for his villainy, and is soon executed handily (manually, by decapitation). The members of the jury then vote to execute themselves, and decide, *nolo contendere,* to forfeit their rights to trial. Following which, as everyone now knows, war ensues. See Chapter 10, "The War of Music." On music generally, see Templar, Simon, *Harmony and All the Rest.* **Q**

Dear Rec. Director;

God Bless that boy Kevin, that "Male Nurse" here at the Home. The Old Grampas are always poking fun at him, calling him a sissy behind his back, & other names. Kevin is such a nice boy, I feel sorry for him, he is the best nurse at the Home even if he is a "Male". I see him pushing Mrs. Vanover around in her wheelchair, talking to her friendly, he treats us like Ladies, opens the door for us, always helpful you know. He tells me he comes from down South, a big family there, he is the oldest. It just breaks my heart to see those Old Codgers razz him so, he is such a good boy.

Yours in Christ,
Enid

P. S. — You don't think he is a homosexual cock sucker fairy like the Old Men say do you?

Ruth calls me, crying. Her young man stood her up, she hates all men. Says her eyes need surgery from all the tears. I say fuck them all, we have our work. Sleep all day in Holiday Inn, then make some calls, people I was in Paris with. That night I go to bar in hotel. Just want alone—not really alone, but with barroom strangers. I drink at bar, talk. Someone named Shafi Baba Kahn pays all my bills. So next day move out to Marriott instead. Beautiful room, suite with marble bath. Tatto asks me to dinner, I say fine, why not. He is tall, ugly Arab. Before we leave, he calls all over the world—Saudi, London, my phone. I don't like, but he's buying dinner. Besides, on the phone I hear him say she is a show-stopper. I feel pretty. Magic clay you buy at Neiman-Marcus takes the old away. He hires limo. We go to all the fancy L.A. clubs. By twelve, he is asleep in back seat and limo has a flat. I get out and help driver and following night go out with him, the driver. Paris friends come. We get wild. I get call from hotel— limo's on my bill. Next day, Raven and I rent car and drive to Santa Cruz. My foot hurts—toothpick I stepped on week after husband died. Went to foot-doctor school. Students didn't get it all out. What the hell, we turn around and go all the way back to L.A. Begin to feel like those old guys, Jack K. and all, on the road. Foot is really bad now. Next day I fly to Tucson to Tasha. Am going to stay for ten days. Tasha has gained weight. She hates me for it. My foot is killing me. Take Tasha and all Tasha's friends to dinner at hotel. Place is jammed with Presbyterian Marriage Encounter Therapy group. All wearing big buttons—*Mary loves Charlie, Eddie loves Carol.* Also, a Herb-a-Life meeting is going on. During day, I hang around downtown Tucson with people who live on bus benches. We drink out of bags. I go to class with Tasha one day, class about anti-Semitism. Teacher says he is an expert on Spanish Jews. Imagine it, an expert on Spanish Jews! Fly home to Chicago. On plane, am so tired, but get off plane and go to club to hear Ruth and Paul. Later on, Paul and I go out for drink. Paul is piano man, black. We do some lines, drink a little lite beer. I wear my necklines slit to waist, my skirts cut to ass. He says to me, "Sharon, you only be a together person if you cut off your head." I am alone. Cold as stone. Call my son, tell him get me drugs from our friendly drugstore man. My foot. Do not worry about me with men. I have learned how to be with them but not be with them. Men. They want relationships, casseroles, movies. I want the slimelight. **Q**

Tom Ahern

STANDING BY TO INTERFACE WITH GODOT

ESTRAGON *and* VLADIMIR *are in a car filled with communications equipment.*

ESTRAGON: The light's green.

VLADIMIR: I know.

ESTRAGON: There's no traffic.

VLADIMIR: I know.

ESTRAGON: Then let's go.

VLADIMIR: We can't.

ESTRAGON: Why not?

VLADIMIR: We're waiting for Godot.

ESTRAGON: Not Godot. He never comes.

VLADIMIR: He'll come. I saw it on the news last night.

ESTRAGON: Last night they did not know about tonight.

VLADIMIR: Last night I taped tomorrow's news.

ESTRAGON: No!

VLADIMIR: Then I fast-forwarded.

There is a beep.

VLADIMIR: It's your beeper! It's Godot!

ESTRAGON: It's not my beeper.

VLADIMIR: The cellular phone?

ESTRAGON (*checking cellular phone*): Not the cellular phone.

VLADIMIR: Modular phone?

ESTRAGON (*checking modular phone*): No.

VLADIMIR: Dictaphone? Modem? Portable stock quote machine?

Beeps continue. They check machines frantically.

ESTRAGON: It's the chicken divan dinner. Open the microwave, in the glove compartment.

VLADIMIR *does. They eat. A message is received on the computer.* VLADIMIR *reads screen with excitement. His eyes tear.* ESTRAGON *reads screen.*

ESTRAGON: "Ga" . . . "ga" . . . *(He looks up.)* Godot?
VLADIMIR: My little girl. Her first electronic words.
ESTRAGON: Aw.
VLADIMIR: Get a pencil. I must write this down.
ESTRAGON: What's a pencil?
VLADIMIR: For God's sake. A narrow cylindrical implement used for writing, consisting of a thin rod of graphite encased in wood or held in a mechanical device.
ESTRAGON: Japanese no doubt.

They wait.

ESTRAGON: Are you sure he said today? Not Friday or Tuesday?
VLADIMIR: Today. Saturday. I heard it with my own earphones.
ESTRAGON: But what Saturday? And is it Saturday? Is it not rather Sunday? Or Wednesday?
VLADIMIR: Call TIME.
ESTRAGON *does.*
ESTRAGON: We have waited many billable minutes for Godot.
VLADIMIR: He owes us nothing. We are not working for Godot, we are waiting for Godot.
ESTRAGON: An existential quibble.

They wait.

ESTRAGON: Now what do we do?

VLADIMIR: I could call someone.

ESTRAGON: You'd tie up the line.

VLADIMIR: We have call-waiting for Godot.

ESTRAGON: You and I don't communicate anymore.

VLADIMIR: We don't share the same data base.

ESTRAGON: We could get local area networking.

VLADIMIR: It's not the same.

ESTRAGON: You could fax a memo to me and I could fax a memo back.

VLADIMIR: That's how my first marriage ended.

ESTRAGON: I'm sorry.

VLADIMIR: She started faxing other men.

ESTRAGON *(reading computer screen):* Eight-forty-five, ten-ten, twelve-twenty . . .

VLADIMIR: They faxed her pictures of jewelry I could never afford.

ESTRAGON: . . . one-forty-five, two-thirty-one . . .

VLADIMIR: She got an electronic mailbox at an undisclosed site.

ESTRAGON: . . . three-thirteen, four-fourteen . . .

VLADIMIR: Reading the Random Numbers Program? I must be boring.

ESTRAGON: The times of airplane departures. Shall we go?

VLADIMIR: We can't. Godot.

ESTRAGON: He never comes.

VLADIMIR: Not today.

ESTRAGON: Let's go.

VLADIMIR: The battery is dead. All the machines. I'll Touch-Tone for help on the cordless.

ESTRAGON: We'll wait. **Q**

!BANANA NITE!

Yung Lung 1990

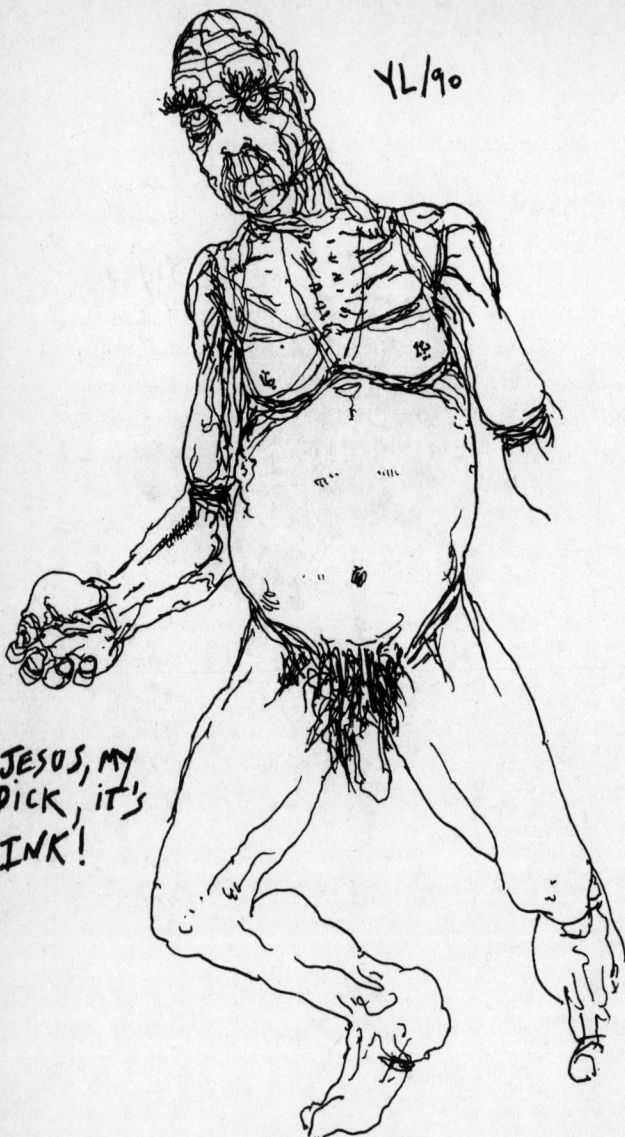

Dear Director of Recreation,

You do so many Good Things for us Old Folks here at the County Home, God Bless + Keep You. The Zoo visit on Mon. was a delight for all of us, I'm saying thank you to "You" from "All of Us." Me + my friend Mrs. Fewkes can't stop talking about the darling puppies, they are so rare + very pretty little things + have such pep + energy which we tired Oldies love to see. Hold-ing it is like my little babies who have forgotten me, when I was a young mother in the Good Old Days. Mrs. Fewkes says we should get a puppy here to keep at the Home for all us Old Ladies to play with, she says when a dog goes into heat it will try to hump anything even an Old Lady like us.

Sincerely Yours,
Mrs. E. J. Crackel

well I am prepaaring to take off earlier tha n I thought to do the cousins book
(the N is fucked up on this typewriter, sorry) , it's going to be a long journey,
there are 18 of us, situated in topeka, burlington Iowa, Killeen Texas, Okolonna
Mississippi, ▬▬▬▬▬▬▬▬▬ dow n in the Florida keys, Jeannnie and
Carolyn, (the Poole girls) ▬▬▬▬▬▬▬▬▬▬▬▬▬▬, and then
the bunch dow n in Poplar Bluff along with Booj who they say sold her tavern
and has gone fairly straight delivering rural mail. and...oh yeah Ro-ro
preaching the Lutheran word of god in Birmingham; I am going to betravelling
with the ma n I was running around with in Montana in October, he bought a
motor home for us to go in, well tow the pickup behind, I told him all we
e needed was a travois and buffalo meat, but ayyhow, it's better than staying
in motels or crashing with the cousins. his name is Jim Johnson but I
refer to him often as Tex add sometimes Lieutenant - Colonel sir. I met him
down at Eminence ad fell in love. It's kind of a relief to fall in love,
you realize you been sort of menntally or emotionally holding your breath for
may years, or maybe shoring something up, rather desperately. And he's a
homeboy so to speak. From south Texas; his daddy was in the army and the
rodeo, so Jim went into the army and avoided the rodeo and made it from
a private in the Texas Guard to Lieutenant Colonel and spetztwpox spent two
years in Vietnam commandinng Vietnamese tropps and was widowed and then
was left with two little kids and so married again and gotx wounded and
several medals for gallantry and then quit at 43 and went to ranching and
raising cattle adx and is axe now out of that thanx to the Farm & Home
Administration or whatever you call it, and he's 57 and he's my man. He
has a degree in either demographic geogrphy or political sciene or both
and taught it at udiversity level for a while. I'm talkinng him into
writinng down his life, he's lived several lifetimes add at least his kids
ought to know about it. So there Susan Marie add I were at Eminence, at
the great underground hillbilly horseg gathering on Jack's Fork, ja 40 miles
northeast of Poplar Bluff in the hills, add we had left her kids with Robbie
Lyn and Judy (cousiss) up near St. Louis and had driven down in the 76
Grand Prix with a shimmy you wouldn't believe, awash in Dr. Pepper bottles
and rag paper from MacDonnald's and we went skidding into the campground,
dodginng mules (there were 1400 people and 2000 horses and 155 mules)

annd fetched up down ᴇ near the river. Susan Marie and I got the tent up and
I lost her in it, she was kind of eaten by the tent for a while. And then we
got our horses from Jim divine, miᴅe was a big red chargy kind of aᴅimal amd
Susann's was built on the lines of a railroad bridge, but anyway, after we
got camp set up late at night I sat down with a candle to ᴡᴀᵻ write a letter
y to you, which I nnever did finish, on account of falling in love and the
wonnderful relief of falling in love, and so I was writing away and crushing
bugs and Susan Marie said, me and this fellow camped next to us is goin to
make a fire, girl, come on and help us. I heard him whistling, he whistles
a lot, cattlemen and horsemenn do that as a habit, it quiets the animals and
leaves a kind of cowboy signature on the air. Don't print this letter. And
he was whistling "There's An Old Spinning wheel I n The Parlor, ' which is the
song my mother sang in sixth grade and she won the silver cup for it, because
she had such a light, pretty voice, that was at Lynn Creek on the Osage.
So I went over there to help and I see this obviously cowboy person drinking
scotch and trying to build a fire out of green oak slabs. So I sat down
across from him and gave a haᴅd, and we got to talking, and he said he was
a rancher, and retired armyᴅ and I kept asking questions and ᶠᶤᵃxz he said
he was in Vietnam, so I wᴇᵼzᵏᵼxz went into a knee=jerk reaction and said,
'well hell, what we need to get this fire going is some <u>Vietnamese huts</u>,
ᶆan, like, you know, how about some napalm, I mean we could just<u>nukᶩe</u> it⅃
so we got into a quiet, fierce fight there for a while and Susan says,
what are you-all taking about and we both said, nothing, honey. She's only
24. And then we sat up all night and he turned me onto Tom Wolfe's Our House
to Bauhaus and The Painted Word, which he later sent to me. And then at dawn
the muᴅles started up and he laid down on a cot and put his hat over his
face and checked out. And the next day Susan Marie and I rode up and down
the trails, and Red charged everywhere he went, I mean cannon fire would have
been meat and drink to Red.   Aᴅd we nearly got run down by the fast ride,
150 horses going at full steam, it was like being run down by a giant ᴇᴘ piece
of farm machinery. Atticus wouldn't have survived. Susan-Marᴂe and I ran
straight into the river to get away from them. And then that night there was
a dance and her b husband Mark came down, he drives for UPS, so he got off
work and came to sit around and ᵼᴉᴇᵼz tell stories by the fire. And they
went to the dance and there I was by myself and sorry I had said cruel things
to the Lieutenant-Colonel and I saw him putting away his daughter's little

quarter horse mare, annd so I we£x went over and said,'hey Tex, don't put tha
t horse away', and so he didn't, and we took off inn the dead of ight down the
big soft roads back into the hills and talked and talked and talked. About
growing up poor and desperate, and mamaging university, and how texans talk
different from Missourians, and demographic geography, and he told me about
Germayy and San Francisco and Saigon, and ranching Brangus cattle, and selling
thigngs off, and falling into things, and then he said,'This little horse is
doing pretty well, I'm goig to ride her into the brush' and went straight up th
side of the hill in the pitch dark. There was no stopping Red, of course, and
I forgot to tell you I was onn bareback, and so Red plunged straight up the
hill after him and the little brown mare, and we got left behidd, so Red sat
back on his hocks and took a flying leap straight uphill. I guess he figured
he could make better ti/me in the air. I don't know how I stayed on. Yes
I do, that horse to this day has deep fingermarks in his undeserving neck.
And then I kind of saw them dissapearing into the timber and had no wish to
be sprung off my horse by a blackjack limb and so searched around and caught
up on the top of the hill where another road was. and thenw e went back and
rode down to the dance and rode right up to the edge where the band was
playigg and the horses did really well. By this time I want this guy like
Sherman wanted Atlanta. So thexx we sat up again all night and talked and
talked about books and etc. and I am thinking this guy nearly got blown to
bits in Vietnam and shot and walked over buy giant cattle and he's been
saved alive just for me. I want him I want him. And then the ex next morning
he's loading his horse and his daughter and going away forever and I ran out
of the tent and demanded his address. And I got it. He's going through a
de;iciously messy divorce, which always spices things up, and but that will
soon be over and now we are going wandering around the south together and
interviewing cousins. He's 5' 4", and very soft-spoken and texan and mean and
romantic. Well, that's my news, after Feb. 1 or thereabouts better get hold me
of me through Susan Marie, we'll d be down around there somewhere,

                love to all,   P.

(hey, you know I wouldn't fall in love with
   no damn poet altho' I tried for years)

FRANCIS LEVY *to* Q

EDIE JENKINS TO BETTY FORD

Edie Jenkins, the star of the television series *Bliss & Marie* and the winner of the 1986 Academy Award for Best Supporting Actress in *Revelry,* has enrolled in the alcohol and drug rehabilitation program at the Betty Ford Clinic. The announcement was made at a press conference called by Miss Jenkins at the Beverly Hills Hotel. Miss Jenkins, whose five previous marriages ended in divorce, will be preparing for both her concert tour and her debut as Mary Tyrone in the revival of Eugene O'Neill's *Long Day's Journey into Night* during her stay at the clinic.

SARIE WILKINS BREAKS DOWN

Morgan and Barbara Wilkins of Elkins Park have announced the breakdown of their daughter Sarie Moore Wilkins. Miss Wilkins, who is also known professionally as Carly, will attend the Menninger Clinic. Her father is an engineer and active alcoholic in Philadelphia, and her mother is on the board of St. Mary's Rehab in Minnesota, where she has also been a patient.

BOB LASH TO SMITHERS

Mr. and Mrs. Tom Lash of Cincinnati gratefully announce the commitment of their son, Bob, to the Smithers Alcohol Treatment Center. Mr. Lash holds the record in rebounding at Kent State, where he served on the varsity from 1953–56. His son, Bob, who recently had a near fatal car accident after driving in a blackout, was also a basketball star at Kent State and is now a forward with the New York Knicks.

Mrs. Lash is the founder of the Will-Do bakery concern, a chain of croissant shops in Ohio.

JOHN DONALDSON ON LEAVE

John Donaldson, senior vice-president of advertising at Kinsley, Moore, the furniture fabrics concern, has taken a leave to enter the drug rehabilitation program at Queens County Hospital. Mr. Donaldson, who is addicted to cocaine and barbiturates and who also has an alcohol problem, is a graduate of the Fashion Institute of Technology. He has had a succession of relationships, all of which have ended in various kinds of failure.

ROBERT ''BUD'' DINE OF TACO WACO IN RECOVERY

Robert Dine, chairman of the board of Taco Waco, has committed himself to Freeport Hospital after a brief but disastrous vacation at Las Brisas. Taco Waco is the largest producer of frozen tacos in the United States.

CARL ABRAHAMS IN PSYCHOANALYSIS

Carl Abrahams, whose company, Loadathon, has been prominent in moving homes, is undergoing psychoanalytic treatment for an as yet unnameable fear, a spokesman announced today. **Q**

Screaming became a public affair

For credit-card orders of back numbers, call toll-free, at 1-800-733-3000. Prices and isbn codes shown below. Or purchase by check or money order via letter to Subscription Office. Note addition of postage and handling charge at $1.50 the copy per each copy requested.

Q1	$6.95	394-74697-x
Q2	$5.95	394-74698-8
Q3	$5.95	394-75536-7
Q4	$5.95	394-75537-5
Q5	$6.95	394-75718-1
Q6	$6.95	394-75719-x
Q7	$6.95	394-75936-2
Q8	$6.95	394-75937-0
Q9	$7.95	679-72139-8
Q10	$7.95	679-72172-x
Q11	$7.95	679-72173-8
Q12	$7.95	679-72153-3
Q13	$8.95	679-72743-4
Q14	$8.95	679-72893-7